A
CHASE
FOR
Christmas

CANDACE SHAW

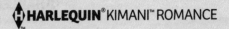

HARLEQUIN® KIMANI™ ROMANCE

Recycling programs
for this product may
not exist in your area.

ISBN-13: 978-0-373-86478-2

A Chase for Christmas

HARLEQUIN®

Printed in U.S.A.

™ www.Harlequin.com

Candace Shaw writes romance novels because she believes that happily-ever-after isn't found only in fairy tales. When she's not writing or researching information for a book, you can find Candace in her gardens, shopping, reading or learning how to cook a new dish.

She lives in Atlanta, Georgia, with her loving husband and their loyal dog, Ali. She is currently working on her next fun, flirty and sexy romance.

You can contact Candace on her website at candaceshaw.net, on Facebook at Facebook.com/authorcandaceshaw, or you can Tweet her at Twitter.com/candace_shaw.

Books by Candace Shaw

Harlequin Kimani Romance

Her Perfect Candidate
Journey to Seduction
The Sweetest Kiss
His Loving Caress
A Chase for Christmas

Visit the Author Profile page
at Harlequin.com for more titles.

Chapter 1

Preston Chase perused the bakery display case and all of the tasty desserts in his view in Sweet Treats Bakery. Everything from decadent chocolate pastries to creative and too-beautiful-to-eat cupcakes seductively screamed his name. His sister was the owner and head pastry chef, so he knew whatever he selected would be delectable. But like his dating life, he couldn't settle on just one.

Glancing up, he met his baby sister's angelic but impatient stare. "Quick rushing me, Tiff. You have any more sweet potato pie?"

Wrinkling her nose, Tiffani Hollingsworth sighed deeply. "No, and I don't want to see another sweet potato *anything* until next Thanksgiving. I think I baked over two hundred of them in the last three weeks. I'm trying to perfect an eggnog-flavored cupcake. Your nephew insists that I do so."

"Mmm, that sounds good. I'll volunteer to do a taste test when they're available, but for now—" he rested his light brown eyes back on the desserts in front of him "—I need something. Everything looks so delicious."

"You *can* have more than one," she suggested. "While you decide, tell me more about your Winter Wonderland project, and how I can assist." Leaving her spot behind the counter, she trekked over to the door, locked it and flipped the sign on the glass to Closed.

A sincere smile reached his face at the mention of his upcoming project for the children at the Coretta Scott King Children's Hospital in downtown Atlanta. Having been a patient there as a child with leukemia, Preston now visited the children there with his service dog, a golden retriever named Hope, who was trained to add a little sunshine to their day.

"I'm having two events on Christmas Eve. One is during the day for the children who can't leave the hospital, and the other is at night for the children who are still patients but go back and forth for treatments as well as the ones who are in remission. My team worked overtime on the planning, and I developed a new video game in honor of the event. Each child will go home with one along with their Christmas wish list choices. That way I can relieve a little stress on the parents."

"You're such a sweetheart," she said as she counted the money and credit card receipts from the cash registers. "I'll donate all the cupcakes and goodies you want."

"Thank you, and I'll have an éclair." He pointed to his favorite dessert and said drily, "Just wanted to try something different." Shrugging, he checked his watch. He needed to head home and prepare for his Friday night date.

Grabbing the tongs, she placed half a dozen into a yellow-and-white-striped box that matched the awning over the door of the bakery. "You select the same dessert every time, Prez." She paused as a sarcastic smirk crossed her face. "Just like your choice in women. They're all carbon copies. And you wonder why you haven't found Mrs. John Preston Chase III yet."

Chuckling at her saying his whole name, Preston slid the box off of the counter. "Sis, when I tried something different—" he nodded his head toward the Paint, Sip, Chat Studio next door "—I got shot down. It's like she's immune to me."

"You can forget it. My best friend just isn't interested," she reminded him. "She prefers someone a little more low-key, not living his day like it's his last."

"I like to be free and spontaneous. You know that. 'Live in the moment' is my motto."

Tiffani smiled sweetly. "I know, Prez. Going through what you did as a child, I can't say that I blame you, but my girl just isn't into you."

"Mmm… I wouldn't say that."

A movement through the window caught his attention, and his eyes rested on the person in question. Blythe Ventura jumped out of a black truck parked between her studio and the bakery and darted around to the bed, where a medium-size Christmas tree lay wrapped in twine. She unlatched the tailgate, pulled it down and tugged on the tree.

Her jeans-clad hips and rounded butt were provocatively accentuated as she slid the evergreen a quarter of the way out before stopping and wiping her brow with the back of her hand. After sighing, she attempted to try again but halted as a frustrated expression crossed her sweet, makeup-free face. Her natural black curls were pulled up into a bouncy ponytail on the top of her head, which enhanced her beauty even more. Huge gold hoops hung from her ears and hit her cheeks every time she shook her head back and forth. Quite a few multicolored bracelets encircled her right wrist. The black sweater fit snug over her perky, plump breasts that jiggled when she tugged on the tree, and his smile grew wider with every passing second at the glorious sight.

Blythe was indeed a sexy, beautiful, independent woman he'd admired from afar for over a year. However, whenever he attempted to flirt or ask her out, she'd laugh as if it was the funniest joke she'd ever heard. And while most of the time he was teasing her, Preston did find her alluring.

Setting the box on the counter, he walked toward the door and unlocked it. "I'll be back." Winking, he left Tiffani shaking her head wearing an oh-boy-here-we-go-again expression.

Sinking his hands in his coat pockets, he strode to Blythe, who started to pull the tree again, only to stop and mumble a curse word.

"Hi there," he started. "Need some assistance?"

She jumped a tad and rested her brown doe eyes on him. "Hey, Preston. I didn't realize you were there." She backed away from the truck. "I'd love some help. Thank you," she answered sincerely in a deep, raspy voice with a Brooklyn accent. "If you get on the bed, I can pull it out while you push."

So many sexual innuendos entered his brain as he pressed his lips together in a smile to keep from sharing them. Usually he tried his best to be a gentleman and respectful with her since she was his sister's best friend. And even though she shot him down, Blythe was always cordial and pleasant with him. They weren't friends per se, but they were cool, and he appreciated her being a great friend to Tiffani.

Glancing at the tree, he saw it wasn't much bigger than the one he'd recently carried into his parents' home. "I'll grab it. You just open the door to your studio and tell me where you need me to place it."

She did as requested, and a few moments later, it stood tall in the window of the lobby. Circling the tree, she cut the twine with a pair of scissors while he stretched the branches out. Afterward they both stood back and admired it.

"It's beautiful," he complimented her. "I see you're falling into the holiday spirit the day after Thanksgiving."

"Yep. I visited Tiffani this afternoon to grab a croissant sandwich, and Christmas music played in the bakery, reminding me I need to decorate the studio." She ran her fingers along the tree. "I love this time of the year. So festive and family-oriented."

"Me, too. Christmas was always a big deal in the Chase household. In fact, my mother had everything set up a few days before Thanksgiving. My parents go all out with the lights on every shrub and mechanical reindeer. My dad says he's going to add a Santa Claus on the roof this year."

"Sounds like my family." Pausing, she turned her attention toward the tree once more. "I sincerely appreciate your help."

"Are you going to decorate it now?"

"No. I teach an art class here on Saturday mornings, and I promised the children last week they could help me."

Preston's brain went into overdrive. "Oh, so you like working with children?"

"Yes. Love them. Especially the little ones. I used to teach art at the elementary and high school levels before opening my studio a few years ago. I miss it sometimes, especially during this time of the year with winter-themed programs, making the extravagant sets and festive costumes for the children."

The wheels in his head began to turn, and he was surprised the thought hadn't crossed his mind before, but he hadn't seen Blythe in a couple of weeks. "Mmm...well, I'm planning a Winter Wonderland project for the children I visit at the hospital. Would you be interested in helping me and my committee make it come to life? I have a vision, but I'm not artistic, as you know from the paint class my family and I participated in with you last year."

She nodded her head. "Yeah, I remember, but your pumpkin didn't turn out too bad."

A sly smile inched up his jawline. "Well, I did have a fantastic teacher, even though it would've turned out better if I wasn't so distracted by her beauty." He stepped into her personal space, and he could've sworn he saw her breath suck in, but she laughed out loud as she always did when he flirted with her.

"Oh, Preston," she replied, patting his chest. "You know your flirting never works on me. Save it for all the other women in Atlanta. However, I'd be happy to help with your project. Sounds like it will be fun."

He was used to her brush-offs, and he still found it amusing that she always had a comeback for him. Sometimes he flirted just to see what witty remark she'd make, and other times he loved to hear her laugh.

"Well, thank you for volunteering to help."

"No problem. My mom had breast cancer years

ago, so I can only imagine what those children are going through. It has to be utterly scary for them."

A heaviness settled in his chest at her words. "It is scary. I've been in their shoes. I had leukemia as a child."

A sadness washed over her features. "Oh… I had no idea," Blythe said emphatically. "No wonder you do so much for the children's hospital."

"Yeah, I was in and out for four years." He stopped when he noticed she still frowned. "Hey, don't look so sad." He comforted her with a smile and pinched her chin. "I'm alive and in amazing health…and quite handsome, may I add." He noticed her expression didn't change even with the joke.

"It just took me by surprise. I didn't know."

"It's one of the reasons I live each day like it's my last… Well, I'm not a daredevil. I do love my life. Plus, my mother would kill me if I died while swimming with sharks or something insane like that."

"I thought Tiffani said you go skydiving every birthday."

He shrugged. "That's not extreme." His eyes landed on a blue storage crate marked Lights sitting on a nearby chair in the lobby area. "Are you going to hang the lights now?"

"I have two paint parties tonight I need to prepare for, and one of my assistants is on vacation. I'll have to do it once I'm closed. I need to have it done before the children arrive in the morning. That way all they have to do is hang the ornaments."

"Nonsense. You don't close until ten. I'll do it for you." Strolling over to the crate, he lifted the lid and saw the lights neatly coiled around a huge hook.

"You don't have to do that. You brought that heavy tree inside for me. I'd still be wrestling with it if it wasn't for you." Her eyebrows raised in an amused manner. "Besides, it's a Friday night. I'm sure you have plans, Mr. Party All the Time."

"I kinda do, but it's no biggie. This won't take long. You just concentrate on setting up for the parties. I'm going to run back to the bakery to grab my box of goodies before Tiffani leaves."

"But…" Blythe shook her head while trying to suppress a smile. "You really don't have to."

He walked over to the door and opened it. He could've sworn he read more into her expression and demeanor. Preston knew a woman's body language. While Blythe had always remained firm and unbothered by him, he wasn't so sure that was the case at the present moment. Now curiosity had him questioning why.

Glancing at her over his shoulder, he cracked a grin at the thought of perhaps winning her over after all. "No worries. I got you."

No worries? The comment had played on repeat in her head for the last ten minutes. How could she not worry when the irresistible Preston Chase graced her lobby, hanging lights on the tree? Blythe walked around the stations, setting a smock on the back of each chair as she heard the giggles of a few ladies walking past in the hallway to the other room, where her assistant Mandi was about to begin class. She also heard catcalls, whistles and "Damn, he's fine." Women were even going back for a second peek at the man who was probably enjoying every moment of their attention.

Prez was a mouthwatering, gorgeous hunk of a man. His broad shoulders, muscular build and, she guessed, six-foot-two height were definitely enough to drive any woman crazy with lust when first laying eyes on him. Not to mention his infectious smile showcasing pearly white, immaculate teeth, smooth butterscotch skin and his silky, curly hair that she sometimes hated to admit that she would love to weave her fingers through. And then there were his lips. Succulent. Sexy. She'd never paid much attention to a man's lips like this before, but there was something about the curve and subtle plumpness of them that made her want to draw them…with her tongue.

Blythe's thoughts drifted to when she'd first met him a year ago at a paint party her new friend and now best friend had arranged for a family outing. Blythe was aware that Tiffani's brother was the creator of the famous *Dart and Drive* video game that had amassed almost half a billion dollars, followed by more popular games. However, she expected a geeky, dorky, nerdy kind of guy with glasses, pants too short and a lisp, for some reason. Tiffani had mentioned that women practically threw themselves at her brother, but Blythe figured it was because he was worth millions. But when she entered the room to begin the party, she had to hold back a gulp and keep her gaze elsewhere. The man exuded a sexiness and confidence on a level that could break the Richter scale and a voice as smooth as caramel. It became worse when he'd roamed his eyes over her and started to flirt; however, she'd managed to remain composed and withstand the temptation to give in to him. His suave manner, good looks and intelligent charm could surely win over any woman's heart, including hers if she wasn't careful.

So why did Blythe keep blowing him off every time he flirted or paid her a compliment? Simple. She'd dated his type before. The player. The woman juggler. The pretty boy type that women sometimes fought over. Sure, he seemed like a nice guy. He loved his family, was overprotective of his sister and her son, KJ, and had a soft spot for the children at the hospital where he volunteered. He was an intellectual and even possessed a tad of nerdiness that she found sexy in a confident man like him. But none of that changed the fact that he was a notorious player.

Once the stations were completed, Blythe had about twenty minutes before the women's group at a church not far from the studio was to arrive. Sighing, she contemplated either staying in the classroom and waiting or venturing back out into the lobby area to greet her class as she always did. A movement out of the corner of her eye caught her attention as a chill ran through her body. She'd thought it was Preston. However, it was her receptionist, Ms. Bernice, standing in the doorway with her arms folded across her ample bosom. The sixty-year-old woman had a slight, curious smile displayed on her face, and her glasses hung down on her nose, her eyes peering over.

"Hey. Didn't know you were here," Blythe said, heading over to her work area and sliding a smock over her sweater.

"Just came back from my dinner break. I see you bought a tree. Did the handsome man come with it? Perhaps I need to go buy a few trees myself," she teased, running her hands through her gray curls.

"Nooo. That's Tiffani's brother, Preston. He saw me struggling with it and offered to help bring it inside."

Ms. Bernice slowly nodded her head. "Oh, I know who he is. I'm just surprised to see him here. You're always brushing that fine young man off. If I was only thirty... I mean, twenty years younger..."

Blythe laughed. "Yeah, you'd be a part of his flock of women. No thank you."

Ms. Bernice turned around to leave but pivoted back. "You only get played by a man if you allow him to do it. Your group is starting to arrive, but they're chatting in the lobby and ogling Mr. Chase. Shall I send them back?"

"No need. I'll be out in a moment. Just want to make sure everything is ready for them."

Ms. Bernice's stare perused the ten stations set up in the middle of the room. "Seems like everything is in place." And with that, she finally left.

Moments later, Blythe headed to the lobby to find the lights on the tree and Preston chatting with two women while looking at a cell phone. *I guess he's getting their numbers*, she thought as she nodded at him and then strolled to the lit Christmas tree. But she was mistaken. Instead, it seemed like he was showing them how to download one of his free video game apps to their phones. The ladies gave him a sexy, sultry thank-you and followed Ms. Bernice down the hall.

"Hey, whatcha think of my light hanging skills?" he inquired, standing next to her.

His masculine, woodsy cologne caressed her nose in an erotic, sensual way, and she stepped up to the tree to straighten a light that wasn't crooked.

"You did a great job. Thank you so much."

"You're quite welcome. You know, I was thinking maybe we should have Christmas trees as a part of the Winter Wonderland."

"That's a great idea, but much taller than this one. Maybe each tree could have a color scheme or something like that."

"Yeah. I know you don't have much time to discuss details now, but my committee is meeting on

Sunday evening. I know it's short notice, and I understand if you can't make it."

"No. I'm off on Sundays, so that's fine."

"Cool." Slipping his cell phone from his pocket, he punched the keypad on the screen and handed her the phone. "Just input your contact information and I'll text you the address."

Once finished, she handed him the phone. He eyed it, typed something and then placed it back into his pocket with a mischievous expression.

Sizing him up, she tapped her chin. "What did you type to make you look at me like that?"

Snickering, he scooped his leather jacket up from a nearby chair and slid it on. Preston stepped into her comfort zone, but this time she didn't have to stifle a gulp. Blythe decided if she was going to work with him on his project, she'd have to keep him even more at bay than usual. She couldn't let him know that his presence unraveled her.

"I added your name to your number," he answered matter-of-factly. "That's all. Why? You think I'm always in bad-boy mode?"

"Uh…no."

Pushing open the door, a few more ladies passed through while running their eyes over him, but his own eyes never left Blythe's face. "Relax, baby girl. I can be nice. I'm not always naughty. Well…unless that's what you want." He bestowed a wicked smile on her and exited.

Blythe remained rooted in the middle of the lobby,

oblivious to her surroundings, as she watched Preston through the glass door. He strolled casually to his black two-door Aston Martin and sped off as if he knew she was watching.

When she finally made it back to her paint session, her thoughts drifted to the upcoming weeks working on the Winter Wonderland project. She hoped her interactions with him would be minimal. If not, she had a feeling Preston was going to be everything but nice.

Chapter 2

Blythe rode the elevator up to the third floor of the huge, updated industrial building on the outskirts of downtown Atlanta. The first two floors served as the offices of JP3 Chase Technologies, Preston's company, and the top floor was his loft apartment. He'd sent a text message with the address and pass code to enter the gated parking lot and the building plus another code for his private elevator. He'd also asked her not to eat dinner because he was having the meeting catered by Q Time Restaurant, a family-owned soul food place that specialized in healthy, home-cooked meals. She'd frequented the eatery and was glad they were catering the dinner.

Once the elevator stopped, she shifted her oversize sketch bag and purse on her shoulder and waited for the doors to open. As she stepped out, panic seared through her veins and she screamed as a large golden dog charged her way and pounced its paws up on her shoulders. It licked her cheek in a sloppy kiss.

"Hope! Down, girl." Preston commanded in a firm voice while grabbing Blythe to him by the waist and wiping her cheek with his hand. "I'm so sorry. She's never done that before," he said, eyeing the dog, who'd lain at his feet with a sulk. "She usually waits until I introduce her to people. Are you okay?" he asked in concern, sliding the huge bag from her and hoisting it onto his shoulder.

Blythe sighed in relief that the dog hadn't bitten her and swiped her hand through her curls. "Oh, yeah. I just wasn't expecting it. That's all. But I love dogs, and I know golden retrievers are highly affectionate. So if she's calm, I'd love to meet her."

"Alright." He patted his knee and the dog stood up. "Hope, this is Blythe. Blythe, this is Hope."

Blythe smiled at the dog with warm brown eyes, who wagged her tail fast back and forth. Blythe petted Hope's head, followed by a friendly ruffle. "Nice to meet you. She's beautiful, Preston. How old is she?"

"Almost two years old and usually well-behaved. I feel bad she jumped on you like that."

"No problem. I'm fine." She followed him into the extravagant, contemporary-style loft divided with brick walls, enormous tapestry drapes and comfy seating areas. There was a huge, restaurant-type kitchen along a wall of windows, where two older women were preparing a delicious-smelling dinner that rumbled her stomach and reminded her she hadn't eaten since breakfast. Nearby was a wooden dining table that appeared as if it could hold twenty people. Hope walked alongside her master for a bit before she veered away and plopped on a huge dog bed in front of the lit fireplace. Preston motioned for Blythe to sit in one of the oversize gray chaise lounges that were the same size as a full bed, and he sat in the one opposite. Curling her legs underneath her, she was grateful for the warmth of the fire, because the temperature outside had dropped that afternoon and she'd forgotten her jacket.

"I'm fine, Preston," she stated once more since he seemed still to be somewhat anxious over the incident. "No need to be upset with her."

"No. She's also a trained service dog and accompanies me to the children's hospital. Hope is usually pretty calm around strangers, so there's something about you she really likes, or you have doggie treats on you," he teased.

Upon hearing her name, the dog's ears perked up, and she set her eyes on Preston while rapidly beating her tail against the mat.

"So, where's everyone else?" Blythe questioned. She'd arrived twenty minutes early because she

wasn't familiar with the area, but she assumed people would show up soon. Unless he'd only invited her,
and she really hoped that wasn't the case. However,
Preston had always treated her with the utmost respect since she was best friends with his sister. Plus,
he didn't seem the type to lure women to his house.

"They should be here soon. You're early." He
paused and nodded to the picture above the fireplace. "Do you like the painting?"

Gazing up, she realized it was one of her favorite abstract pieces that she'd painted. Wrinkling her
forehead, she turned toward him. "Where did you
buy that? I gave it to Tiffani when she requested
some pieces for a couple of charity auctions."

"The scholarship fund-raiser that Tiffani's soror-
ity had at the beginning of the summer. I'd wanted
both pictures, but my cousin-in-law Elle outbid me.
But that's fine. I love this one more. It's peaceful. I
relax here after a long day with a brain tired from
developing new game concepts and strategies. Staring up at the serene mixture of blues and greens is
quite tranquil. It's calming, and sometimes I need
that. It gives my eyes a break from staring at computers all day."

"Mmm-hmm. You definitely understand the
mood I was in. I painted it after a peaceful time of
unwinding and meditating. The one Elle won was
the opposite with bold, daring colors and somewhat
of a wild streak. I was listening to one of my Miles

Davis CDs. The songs during his jazz fusion period. Insane, up-tempo jazz that made sense only to him, but I understood the emotions behind it. I'm almost surprised you like this one better. The other one seems more your speed."

"Yeah, I know you think I'm all play, but I work hard, so I play hard. Live in the moment. It's been my motto for a long time."

She nodded in agreement, thinking of the wild stories Tiffani had mentioned about him. "So I've heard, playboy."

He chuckled. "You know, I don't really consider myself a playboy or a player. I just date and have fun. Women usually approach me. But eventually, I do want to settle down with a wife and have children. I was raised by two parents who have a loving, wonderful marriage. I want the same. Sometimes I go on one or two dates and realize the woman simply isn't the one for me and there's no point of wasting my time or hers. And for the record, I don't sleep with every single one of them, but I do like to have fun and live life like it's my last day. That doesn't always include being with a woman. At times, I travel alone, skydive, play video games or find something new to experience."

Blythe was about to respond, but the opening of the elevator doors sent both of their attentions to it, and Preston excused himself to greet a group of men and women. Releasing the breath that had been lodged in her windpipe, she was relieved that the other committee members were beginning to arrive. She noticed Hope stayed seated and watched her instead. Blythe kneeled down and rubbed Hope's head before the dog turned over on her back and placed her paws up.

"Oh, I know what you want," Blythe said in a singsong voice, rubbing the dog's stomach. "Who's a good girl?" Blythe loved dogs and had been searching for one lately. It had been two years since her beloved Misty, a German shepherd, had died. Perhaps a sweet golden retriever puppy was what she needed for Christmas.

Preston returned as several of the guests made their way into the dining area.

"I see you two are becoming fast friends." Preston stooped down and rubbed the dog's head.

"I love dogs. I lost my dog of thirteen years a few years ago, but I'm contemplating owning another one. I think I'm ready, but I'll always love and miss my Misty."

"Sorry to hear that. Dogs are truly a man's…and a woman's best friend. What breed do you want?"

"Actually, a retriever like Hope or a Labrador would be ideal. Something sweet and lovable so people won't be scared of my dog. Misty was a German shepherd, so sometimes she had to stay in my bedroom when certain family or friends stopped by to visit. I see Hope loves to be spoiled."

Preston nodded his head with a smirk. "She loves tummy rubs and her hair being brushed. She's a pampered pooch. Aren't you, girl?"

"All women loved to be pampered."

He raised a questioning eyebrow. "Really?" He stood and reached his hand down to her.

She grabbed it but let it go quickly once she was back on her feet. The warmth of his hand was cozy and comfortable. For a moment, it felt nice to hold a man's hand, even if the man was Preston.

"Well, I know I do," she admitted. "Facials, pedicures and of course, deep tissue massages. That should be at the top of every woman's pampering list."

He glanced at her over his shoulder. "I'll keep that in mind," he answered in a low, seductive voice.

Ignoring the heat that rose to the surface of her skin, Blythe stopped walking as her eyes perused the loft. "Where's your powder room? I just need to wash my hands." *And have a moment to calm the hell down.*

"Down that hallway. The last bedroom on the left has a bathroom. The others are still being renovated. Use whatever you like."

"Thank you."

Making her way down the hall, she realized that only the front part of the apartment was lofty. The rest was divided into rooms, and she peeked into each that was open as she passed. A home office, two bedrooms, a game room with a pool table along with vintage video game machines, and a workout room. Finally she landed in front of the one he'd mentioned. She stepped into a vast bedroom that was more than likely the master. An oversize cherry wood bed with gigantic swirled poles was the focal point of the room, draped in a plush gold comforter topped with at least a dozen decorative throw pillows.

That must be where the magic happens, she thought sarcastically.

Peering around, she spotted a door by the sitting area and made her way in its direction. Behind it was indeed the bathroom, and just like the rest of his home, it was immaculate. The window scarf that flanked the huge stained glass window over the garden tub matched the comforter and the drapes from the bedroom. A flat screen hung on the wall above the tub and there were two vanities on opposite brick walls. She trekked to the one that was empty except for a gold tray with hand napkins and a matching soap dispenser. The other one held colognes, a few pictures of the Chase family in gold frames and an electric toothbrush and toothpaste.

Glancing at herself in the mirror, she noticed her flushed face and sighed. She had no idea what had come over her. Preston Chase had always flirted with her and teased her. She had never taken him seriously and would easily brush him off with a laugh and not give it a second thought. But now her nerves were unraveling and she had to get herself together. He wasn't someone she could ever in a million years date, not even one date. He was the kind of man she avoided.

Ever since her ex had repeatedly cheated on her three years ago, she'd distanced herself from players like him and Preston. She still dated but thanks to a string of dating disasters lately, she'd decided to take a break and reevaluate her life. While the occasional outing would arise, she wanted the next man she dated to be long-term and one day lead to marriage.

It sure as hell wasn't going to be Preston Chase. The thought made her nearly laugh out loud. She couldn't even imagine him married and definitely not to her. She could envision him with children, perhaps because he loved and doted on Tiffani's son as if he was his own. What kind of woman would he end up with, anyway? Would he want an independent working woman who was his equal or a trophy wife at his beck and call?

Realizing she'd been away for almost five minutes, Blythe tossed the napkin into the wastebasket on the side of the vanity, checked her hair and headed back to the meeting.

She returned to the dining area, where the other committee members were loading their plates with food and conversing about their day or the project. A few other people had arrived and were sharing ideas with Preston in the kitchen. He glanced in her direction when he noticed she'd returned, and a warm smile reached his face. Turning her attention away from him, she chatted with a few people she'd met at a party at Tiffani's home. There was something intriguing about Preston that sent a slew of goose bumps along her skin. Even though there were twenty other people in the room, she sensed that his attention was solely on her. The thought scared her, and she laughed at herself for having that silly and ludicrous notion. She wasn't even the man's type. He was just being friendly as always because she was his sister's best friend.

Satisfied with that realization, Blythe made a plate with roasted herb chicken, collard greens, cornbread dressing and a hearty helping of peach cobbler on a saucer. Moments later, everyone was seated around the dining table as Preston made the introductions and informed the committee members of each other's roles for the project. A lot of preparations had already been made, but the most important was coming up with the design plans, according to Preston's vision. She was paired to work with Devin Montgomery, the owner of Supreme Construction, whom she'd already spoken with briefly that morning about the event, and his wife, Sasha, who was in charge of the Christmas trees and their decorations.

For the next three hours, Blythe, Devin and Sasha worked together in Preston's game room, and the other subcommittees broke off in different areas, as well. Preston was in and out, checking on them and offering his suggestions. Blythe was impressed by his expertise on the design plans, and his intellect showed through. For a moment, he wasn't the flirtatious man she was used to. Instead he was serious, confident and compassionate about the Winter Wonderland project. He wanted the best, most extravagant event possible for the children who had grown near and dear to him, and cost wasn't an issue.

The Montgomerys called it a night, citing that they needed to relieve the babysitter, and Blythe needed to leave, as well. When they emerged from the game room, they spotted Preston by himself on the lounge in front of the fireplace, working on his laptop. He turned his attention toward them as they entered the great room.

"You guys were brainstorming for a long while. Everyone else has left, but I'm really excited about all of the ideas you've come up with. I'm glad you were able to put my crazy vision on paper."

Devin nodded. "My crew and I will start building the set in the morning, Prez."

"And since I'm off on Mondays, I'll be able to begin one of the murals tomorrow, as well," Blythe said, pulling her keys from her purse.

"Perfect. I'll swing by in the afternoon if I'm done working out the bug in this new game." Sliding the computer off his lap, Preston grimaced and stood to join the trio, who were nearing the elevator.

"Blythe, I needed to discuss one more matter with you concerning the different stations at the event."

"Sure." *Wait, what?*

She bid goodbye to the Montgomerys. Preston continued to chat with them for a few moments more before joining her on the opposite lounge.

"So, I'm ecstatic about all of the stations the children can go to. Tiffani is doing a cupcake decorating station, and I was wondering if you would consider having an art station similar to your paint parties, minus the wine, of course. Maybe two thirty-minute-long sessions?"

"Oh, sure, I can do that. No problem. Perhaps I can do one during the day with the children at the hospital."

Blythe loved the way his face lit up with sincerity and delight at the mention of the children.

"Perfect. They would love that. Maybe you could come with me beforehand to meet them. I'm going next week for story time."

"I'd love to. Just text me the information, and if I don't have a paint party, I'll meet you there."

The video game he'd been working on chimed, and they both glanced in the direction of his laptop sitting at the end of his chaise. He sighed and set the computer back on his lap.

"Still working out the kinks, huh?"

"Yeah. It's complete, but just one level has a bug that keeps messing up the other levels after it. It's for the game cartridge the little girls at the event will take home along with the new at-home console that comes out this year and whatever else is on their wish lists for Christmas. The one for the boys is good to go. I'll be up late tonight working. I have a test group on Tuesday, so it has to be done. You wanna play it? Give me some feedback?"

"Sure."

He slid over next to her and set the computer on her lap. He was so close to her that she almost froze. His scent was fresh and manly. She stifled a gulp when he leaned his chest on her back and touched a few keys on the computer to restart the game. The sweater he wore didn't disguise his hard chest resting on her, and even though he was explaining the concept of the game, she hadn't understood a word he'd said. Instead, she was focused on the simple tasks of breathing and keeping her eyes situated on the computer screen.

"There will be a similar game available for a free download on phones, tablets and computers, but it won't be available until the spring. Only the children at the events will receive the cartridges and a free download to their tablets along with five new games my educational division has developed for primary and intermediate grades. Those are the types of games I usually give them, because as the son of two educators, I understand the value of education. However, I do know they need to have a little fun, so I throw in the fun games, as well. That way the kids think I'm a cool dude."

"That's very nice of you." She slid over to the middle of the chaise before she found herself too comfortable against him.

"Well, it gives them something constructive to do and take their minds off the pain they're in. Trust me, it's a horrible feeling."

His face scrunched up for a quick second, and Blythe had the urge to reach out to caress his cheek. Shocked by her thought, instead, she nodded in understanding because she'd witnessed her mother go through some tough times during her cancer period. She could only imagine what Preston and his family had gone through when he was a child. Now she understood why Tiffani always acted like a mother hen with him even though he was the oldest.

She began to play the game while Preston watched and offered hints to her.

"This is a cool game," she complimented him after playing for thirty minutes. She was hooked and almost didn't want to stop. She rarely played the games on her phone, but this one was going to be downloaded as soon as it was available to the public. "Little girls love to play dress-up, so the fact that they can change outfits according to the occasion and win points to buy more cute clothes is pretty sweet."

"Thank you, Blythe. I asked Tiffani, aka girlie-girl, her opinion, and she said the same."

"I see you even have a cupcake shop in the game," she noted with a pleased smile, handing the laptop back to him after completing the first three levels.

"Shout out to my baby sis." He placed the computer on the floor, but he didn't move from his spot next to her.

Blythe was glued to the seat. She wanted to move. Needed to move. He was so close she could hear his pulse race. Or maybe it was hers. She was surprised that she wasn't uncomfortable, especially when he bit his bottom lip lightly in a sexy manner that tied a tangled knot in her stomach. Being alone with him wasn't scary, and that ironically swept a fear into her. Preston was a man she'd kept at bay for the past year. She'd shrug or groan whenever his sister teased her about hooking them up because she knew the notorious millionaire playboy would break her heart. And not necessarily on purpose. Preston was an up-front man, and she was sure that all his female friends, acquaintances, booty calls, girls-of-the-month or whatever he called them were aware he wasn't going to commit to them. Not a road she wanted to go down again, which was why she hadn't had a steady boyfriend in almost three years.

Abruptly she stood, and so did Hope, who'd been napping on her mat. Blythe gave the dog's head a pat as she heeled beside her.

"Leaving?" he asked with a slight frown.

"Yeah. It's been a long day."

Standing, he grabbed her sketch bag from beside the chaise, and they headed toward the elevator. "I understand. I appreciate your help with the project. Hope and I will walk you to your truck. I need to take her outside."

"Thank you, but the truck isn't mine. I borrowed it from a friend so I could haul the tree. Unfortunately, he couldn't help because he had a business meeting, so I'm glad you were there."

His eyebrow rose. "Oh? A boyfriend?" he asked, grabbing Hope's leash from a hook by the elevator and snapping it onto the ring on the dog's collar.

"No, no boyfriend. He's just a good friend," she explained while silently laughing at his curiosity.

"Mmm-hmm. As beautiful as you are, I'm sure he wants more than just a friendship."

Suppressing the heat that wanted to rise so badly on her cheeks thanks to his compliment, she shook her head once more. "No…well, maybe at first," she admitted. "We did go on a date once two years ago, but we realized that there was no romantic connection. We've been cool ever since. He's like a big brother."

"Ah, man. He got placed in the big brother category." He chuckled and pressed the button. A mischievous grin reached across his face as they stepped onto the elevator. "So, you do date?" He pushed the button for the ground level, and the doors closed.

"Yeah. Why do you think I don't?"

"Well, the few times I've seen you at events with Tiffani, I just thought you didn't date because you're usually alone. And when men approach you, you kind of brush them off." He paused as a sly fox smirk inched up his face. "Unless…you don't like men? Is that why you're the only woman not throwing yourself at me?" he teased. "That would explain a lot."

Twisting her lips to the side, she playfully pinched his arm. "I like *men*, but dating is hard for me."

"You had your heart broken?"

"No, not really. More like a wakeup call." She shrugged and paused, contemplating whether or not she should tell him about her horrible ex. "I'm taking a dating break right now. Sure, I've been on a few random dates here and there but for the most part I'm just concentrating on me. Plus, sometimes men want to rush me after the first or second date … if you know what I mean and I'm like 'Dude, slow down. We just met.' That turns me off. Some men want to play games and I'm too old for that. I want forever, not a one-night stand or a relationship that goes nowhere. I want stability and commitment. For some reason I keep meeting duds, so now I'm just taking a break and focusing on me."

He nodded his head in understanding, The doors opened to the first-floor lobby of his company, and they headed out the back door toward where she'd parked.

"Oh…well. Those men are stupid, because you're

a really great person. When men are ready to settle down with the right woman, they'll realize it's not a game. Trust me. I've had a lot of fun times with women and my life in general. But as men we need to know when to respect a woman and her wishes. Apparently these men you've gone out with aren't looking for forever because if they were you wouldn't have had a string of dating disasters. A man who really wanted to be with you would wait, get to know you and respect your decision. Until you're both ready."

Tilting her head, she slid her tote bag from his shoulder and grabbed her keys from the side pouch as they made it to her black four-door Lexus.

"Oh...wow... I..." She pushed the button on the key fob to unlock the door, but she didn't open it. She held the handle and stared up at him in bewilderment.

"What? The last words you thought I'd ever utter?"

"Um...something like that."

"I'm not a bad guy, Blythe," he said in a low, serious tone, stepping toward her. He reached over to the handle, settling his hand on hers, and opened the door for her.

The brief touch of his warm skin in the cold air sent a heated current through her, and the atmosphere around them altered. But she knew she had to ignore it and stay focused. "I know you're not. Your advances and flirtations just don't do anything for me." She laughed and slid into the driver's seat. "Good night, Preston."

"Good night, and thank you for committing to the Winter Wonderland project."

"No problem. I think what you're doing for the children is wonderful. I'm happy to help."

"Ideally you'll get to see another side of me."

"I'm already seeing it." Winking, she pulled the door shut and waved at him through the glass.

She zoomed away a little faster than normal. It was the only way that she could clear her mind until she arrived home. There she could blast some jazz and paint away her crazy thoughts that she could actually have a relationship with Preston Chase.

Chapter 3

Preston poured himself a huge mug of black coffee and scanned his eyes over the computer code on his laptop one last time. He'd stayed up most of the night troubleshooting the bug and playing the game to verify it was fixed. Finally, at three o'clock in the morning, it was complete and he'd crashed in the bed. He knew he should've had the minor issue completed by midnight, but the conversation with Blythe hadn't left his brain. It had wrecked his train of thought, but he was pleased to know that she wasn't one of those women who'd sworn off men because of a broken heart. She wanted a real relationship. A committed, monogamous relationship. The thought irked him even though he wanted the same for himself. However, he had a hard time deciphering whether or not a woman honestly cared about him or cared about his millions and what he could do for them. He figured it was the latter because a lot of them had requests for expensive items after the first few dates. One woman had the audacity to ask for a Range Rover. Needless to say he never called her back. Preston didn't mind spending his money, he was a very giving person, but he did mind being taken advantage of. Perhaps like Blythe, he needed a dating break as well, he joked to himself.

Sipping his coffee, he set the mug on the kitchen island and bit into the bagel topped with cream cheese and capers. He thought about the last real girlfriend he'd had, three years ago. They were exclusive for almost two years. They got along and the sex was awesome. But the emotional chemistry, compassion and connection weren't there. No matter how hard he'd tried. During that stage in his life, he'd figured it was time to settle down and start a family. He'd assumed that since they'd been together longer than any of his previous relationships, perhaps she was the one. However, he couldn't fall in love with her, and in the end they both knew it wouldn't work. Preston wanted to experience the kind of love and respect that his parents shared over the last forty years. It exuded from them, and he desired the same.

Preston shut the laptop, slid the computer into its bag and took one last sip of his coffee before hustling toward the elevator with Hope on his heels.

It was almost noon and he had yet to go down to the offices of JP3 Chase Technologies. Once he arrived at ground level, he walked briskly to his office, waving and nodding at a few of his employees who were heading out to lunch. He waved at his assistant, Linda Jones, who was on the phone, talking fast and aggressively. He plopped into his chair as Hope pounced on her nearby mat. Moments later, Linda peeked her head into the doorway.

"Hey, Boss. Going to lunch with the hubby. Want me to grab something for you?"

"Nah. I just had breakfast."

Wrinkling her brow, she slipped her keys from her purse and leaned against the doorjamb. "I can only assume you were up all night working on the bug."

"Yep, but I got it worked out, so we're good for the test group tomorrow, and then it can be sent for manufacturing and back in time for the event." He opened the program once more and perused it. He knew it was perfect, but one more glance couldn't hurt. He was a perfectionist, especially when it came to his games. There could be no mistakes.

"I figured it would work out." She turned on her heel to leave but pivoted back toward him. "Ms. Ventura stopped by this morning to pick up the check for her supplies."

At the mention of the reason why he could barely sleep last night, Preston drew his focus from the computer and put it back on his assistant, who was more like his second mother.

"Blythe was here?" Standing, he wandered to his minifridge, snagged a bottled water and poured it into Hope's water bowl.

"Yep, she was on her way to the warehouse where she buys paint supplies wholesale and then on to the event venue. Oh, and Devin called. He said everything is going well thus far."

"Good. I'm going to stop by after my meeting with the design team for next year's game ideas." Even though now he wanted to cancel it and head on over to the Winter Wonderland site.

"It was a great idea to add Ms. Ventura to the committee. Tiffani is always praising her artistic abilities, and she seems like a lovely woman. I'm looking forward to seeing her winter-themed murals. I loved the idea of the ice-skating penguins. The crew has the Sheetrock ready for the first one."

"Yeah, she's very creative."

"I saw you checking her out last night."

Preston chuckled. He wasn't surprised that Linda mentioned that. "Well, she's a beautiful and lovely woman. I always check her out. There's something about her I've always admired, but she doesn't take me seriously because of, well…you know the party-guy, playboy rumors."

Twisting her lips, Linda said sarcastically, "Yes, there are those pesky rumors."

"Okay, so they aren't necessarily rumors, but you know I'm a good guy. I've just been having fun with my life, but it doesn't mean I don't want to be with the one. Mrs. Chase is out there. She just hasn't crossed my path yet. But when she does, I'm sure I'll find out it's all about my money."

"Or maybe she has, and you just haven't realized it…or she hasn't realized it. Trust me, there's a woman out there who will love you for you. You're a great, caring man. I'm going to skedaddle so I can be back in time for the meeting."

"Alright. See you in a few. Tell Mr. Jones I said hello."

After Linda left, he leaned back in his chair and let their brief yet insightful conversation sink in. Was she implying that Blythe could possibly be the one? He wasn't sure about that, but he did find her and her artsy ways intriguing. Her different hairstyles always piqued his interest. They ranged from punk rock to braids to afro puffs, her soft natural curls sometimes blown out straight down her back, not to mention an array of colors like purple or blue intertwined in. Her earthy-bohemian fashion selections that included tie-dyed shirts, ripped jeans and eclectic flowy maxidresses and skirts were always sexy on her curvy frame.

She was down-to-earth, intelligent and just about the nicest and most compassionate woman he'd ever met. Her low, raspy voice had a way of capturing his full attention whenever she spoke, leaving him mesmerized. The effect she had on him was uncanny, and the fact that he was attracted to everything about her scared him a tad. Usually he never went too deep with a woman because he didn't want to get too close if he knew it was going to be a fling or relationship that wasn't going to lead to marriage. But Blythe Ventura had pulled at his attention for over a year, and now perhaps it was seriously time to find out why, beyond the fact that he found her gorgeous and sexy.

After the meeting, Preston walked Hope to her fenced-in green area for some playtime before dropping her off in the loft. She usually went everywhere with him, but because of the construction of the Winter Wonderland, he didn't want to risk the chance of her stepping on a nail or otherwise getting hurt.

Pulling up to the event venue, he spotted the ice-skating rink being set up on the side of the building. He parked next to Blythe's Lexus and grabbed his jacket from the passenger seat before heading toward the entrance.

He waved and gave a thumbs-up to the crew outside. "Looking good. Thanks for volunteering."

The transformation of the vast warehouse was amazing, but he'd known Devin and his crew would have it together. They built million dollar homes in the Southeast, so Preston knew this event would be a piece of cake. Some of the men were on a break while a few others were putting the final touches on their assignments. He spotted Devin and Sasha conversing, and paint fumes led his attention to Blythe, who was seated on the floor, painting. He wanted to head straight toward her, but Devin waved in his direction, and Preston mustered a fake smile as he approached the couple.

"Hey, man. Things are really shaping up," he complimented Devin, shaking his hand. "I'm impressed."

"Yeah. I told you my boys got this."

"Well, I see my vision coming to life, and it's amazing."

Preston's eyes scanned the makeshift walls painted white to give Blythe a blank canvas. He briefly glanced in her direction again and tried to concentrate on what Sasha was explaining about Santa's Village and the train for the children to ride. However, all he could focus on was the beauty bobbing her head to the music in her purple headphones while painting penguins ice-skating. The loose-fitting khaki cargo pants did nothing to hide her shapely curves. He was somewhat disappointed that her hair was tied in a scarf because he was curious to see what unique style it was in. She halted midstroke and slowly turned her head in his direction. She didn't seem too surprised as she smiled and waved before returning to the penguin wearing a pink ballerina skirt. *How did she know I was here?*

"I'm glad everything is to your liking," Devin stated. "We've been here since six this morning and are about to call it a day, but we'll be back at the same time tomorrow to build the North Pole and Santa's Village and finish up a few other things."

Sasha glanced at her iPad. "The Christmas trees

are arriving Wednesday morning, so I think by Friday you will definitely see your vision taking shape."

Preston nodded. "Oh, I see it now. I really do." His gaze sped past Sasha and onto Blythe, who'd stood and stretched her arms out along with a yawn. *Is she leaving, as well?*

"The arcade games, merry-go-round and Ferris wheel will arrive two days before the event," Sasha continued, wearing a bright smile as she gazed at her husband.

Preston looked back and forth between the doting couple, who seemed to have forgotten he was there. "Am I missing something? Or is this an inside joke for married folks?"

Devin chuckled and patted Preston on the back. "Nah, man. We have this thing about Ferris wheels. She's just giddy about one being here."

Sasha hooked her arm around her husband's. "We fell in love on one…on our second date, and when we got back together after being separated for five years, we made up on one, and he proposed to me on top of one. It's just special to us." She paused as Devin kissed her tenderly on the cheek. "But getting back to the event. Everything is pretty much on schedule."

"Perfect. You two are wonderful. I'm going to explore. Thank you for your hard work and dedication thus far. This is really shaping up."

"No problem, man. We both want to put a smile on the children's faces. We'll see you tomorrow,"

Devin said as he and Sasha departed from the conversation.

Preston walked around a bit and noticed each area was roped or taped off according to the plans. The game and activity stations, the train tracks throughout, the merry-go-round area and the photo booths were all as he'd envisioned them, and he couldn't wait to see the children enjoying themselves. When he finally made it to his true destination, he found Blythe sipping from a Starbucks cup and sitting crisscross on the floor. Maybe she wasn't leaving just yet. She removed her headphones and placed the cup next to her.

"Hey, Prez. Like what you see?"

"Is that a trick question?" A wicked smile inched across his face. "Do you really want me to answer that?"

"Do you ever quit?" she teased.

He lowered his head and his voice. "Do you want me to?"

Laughing sarcastically, she shook her head. "You're a mess."

"So that's a no, because you shook your head."

Smacking her lips, she turned her eyes away from him momentarily. "Do you like the mural?"

"Yes, I love it. The ice-skating penguins are cute. I'm sure the children will love it, as well."

"I just hope I can finish this tonight. I won't be able to come back until Wednesday to do the polar bears skiing in the Alps on the opposite wall."

"I can help."

Tilting her head, she tried suppressing a smile that turned into a cute smirk. "You're not dressed to paint." Her eyes roamed over his gray dress slacks and blue sweater.

"I can take the sweater off, and I've had these pants for years. No biggie if they get some paint on them." He shrugged, glancing around as Devin and his crew began to leave. "Besides, you'll be here alone soon, and I wouldn't want anything to happen to you. Everyone here is my responsibility."

"We're not in a dangerous neighborhood, but I appreciate the help." Standing, she faced him. "I think I have an Atlanta basketball cap in the car. Wouldn't want to get paint in your hair, pretty boy." Reaching her hand up, she ran her fingers through his silky curls, winked and sashayed away.

"Alright, woman," he called out. "Don't start nothing you can't handle."

She continued walking but looked at him over her shoulder. "Well, that's something we'll never find out. However, I'm sure I would do just fine. It's been a while, but I'm not inexperienced."

The image that conjured up in his head of them naked and laid out in front of his fireplace shocked the hell out of him. He was supposed to be focusing on the project, not flirting with Blythe to the point of wanting to know just how experienced she was.

The heat rising to her cheeks had to be noticeable as Blythe made it to the car. The cold air that hit her face did nothing to cool or calm her down. Had she really just flirted back with Preston? Did she really run her fingers through his hair? What the hell had she been thinking? And then she'd had the audacity to agree to let him assist her in painting. Sure, she was behind and needed the extra help, but she'd planned to call Mandi or her other assistant Allison to see if they had some free time that evening since Paint, Sip, Chat was closed on Mondays. She'd figured the girls could use some extra Christmas shopping money and was about to call them when Preston and his sexy curls approached.

Popping the trunk, she found the hat and noticed cars and trucks of Supreme Construction workers driving away. The ice-skating rink company had arrived around the same time as she had, but the sun was setting, so no doubt they would leave soon, as well. She waved goodbye to the Montgomerys as she trekked back inside while praying that she could concentrate on the task at hand. Being in such proximity to Preston wasn't going to be easy, especially now that she'd actually responded to him. That was a big no, and she couldn't do that again. He was her best friend's brother, and she couldn't cross that line. But his cologne was pure torture and wreaked havoc on her. Ideally the paint fumes would drown out his tantalizing scent.

Upon entering the lobby area, she locked eyes with Preston as he spoke on his cell phone. She stifled a huge gulp and managed to keep her gaze on

his face and not on his bulging tanned arm muscles on display. He'd mentioned earlier taking off his
sweater in order to paint, and he had. Now, thanks
to the flimsy white T-shirt that showcased his tight
abs, she was able to be even more frustrated with
his presence. Handing him the hat, she skedaddled
back to the penguins and set up the task she needed
him to do. Afterward she continued sketching out
another penguin ice-skating. Ten minutes had passed
and still no sign of Preston. Perhaps he had a date
and decided to leave. However, she caught him out
of the corner of her eye, approaching her wearing a
charming smile.

"I'm back. Had to ask Linda to check on Hope for
me. It's almost her dinner and outdoor time."

"Too bad you didn't bring her. She's a sweetheart."

"Yeah, that's my girl. So, what do you need me
to do?"

Stop being so damn handsome, she thought. *And
nice.*

"Follow me."

He did as instructed until they ended up in front
of the scene that she'd sketched out earlier before
he'd arrived to check on the progress.

"The three penguins standing on the snow and
drinking hot chocolate. Think you can paint those?"

"No problem. What color should their hats and
scarves be?"

She pointed to one of the scarves. "If you look
closely, you'll see I noted the color in pencil. The

paints and the brushes are already laid out." She nodded her head to the nearby table covered with a tarp.

"Cool. I promise to stay in the lines."

"I'm sure you will. I'm going back over here to finish the skating penguins. Let me know if you need anything."

They worked in silence, and she was grateful. She'd glance at him every now and then, amused at his full concentration on making sure he was indeed staying in the lines. She was impressed by his attention to detail and the fact that he was doing a great job. When he attended the paint party last year, she'd noticed he was very adamant about his painting being perfect. And even though he wasn't an artist, he was still an artistic and creative person, and it showed through in the over-the-top graphics on his video games.

After a while, the silence became irritating because she'd grown accustomed to painting to music. She decided to tell him about an idea she had.

"Prez, I was thinking since the children know Hope, I could add her to one of the murals. Maybe on one of the small stand-alone walls in Santa's Village. That way you can keep it afterward."

He turned his head toward her, and a sincere and delicious smile formed on his face. *Dang it, maybe I should've sent it in a text message at a later time*, she thought. The man was absolutely glowing with happiness at her suggestion, making him scrumptious all of a sudden.

"I love that idea. Do you need Hope to pose for you?"

"Um…no, but if you have pictures of her, that would be great."

"Sure, I'll text them to you and perhaps take a few more when I get home."

"Thank you." She stopped painting and strolled over to him. He'd just finished one of the penguins. "That's looks awesome. You're a pro, Prez."

"Thank you. You know, we may be here awhile. How about I order some dinner for us and have it delivered? It's almost six o'clock, and I haven't eaten since lunch."

"That sounds great. I don't know this side of town, so I'm not sure what restaurants are over here."

"Not a problem. I'll have one of my assistants pick it up." He set the paintbrush down and pulled his cell phone from his pocket. "So, just pick any restaurant in the city. Do you like Ruth's Chris Steak House? I'm in the mood for surf and turf. I may order something from there for me, but wherever you want is fine."

"Oh…okay." For a second, she'd forgotten the man was a multimillionaire with access to anything he wanted at any time he wanted it. She was thinking pizza, maybe a burger, with a soda in a red Solo cup. He was thinking steak and lobster with champagne in a crystal glass.

"I like steak…um…so that's fine." She shrugged nonchalantly.

"You hesitated. What would you like? It's on me."

"Honestly, I was going to order a pepperoni pizza with a salad from the pizza place I passed around the corner before you showed up. They deliver."

"Done. I'll be back." He punched some numbers on his cell phone screen and jetted toward the lobby area.

She strolled back to her part of the mural and prayed he would be gone for a while so she could catch her breath and think straight. Preston Chase was becoming more and more of a distraction to her. In the past few days, she'd seen and conversed with him more than she had in the year she knew him. They weren't friends. He was just Tiffani's big brother. On the occasions when she did see him, it was only for a few moments. He'd compliment or flirt with her, and she'd brush him off and not think about him until the next time she saw him or his sister mentioned him. And now here she was, working on his project and getting to know the man Tiffani always said he was. Considerate. Compassionate. Caring. Blythe figured of course he was those things to his family because he loved and cared about them, but for the last few days, she was seeing him act that way to others, as well. But that didn't mean she was going to act upon the possibility that she had an innocent curiosity crush on him. *Crush?* she thought as she laughed out loud. *I'm a grown, thirty-year-old woman. I don't have a crush on him. Besides, his niceness doesn't erase the fact that he is a bachelor who loves his playboy lifestyle.*

He returned moments later. "Hey, there. My assistant should be here in about an hour with our food. I figured we could eat in the lobby area since it smells like paint fumes in here."

He picked his paintbrush up and started on the next penguin. She just hoped he'd put his sweater back on while they ate. His muscles flexed every time he stroked the paintbrush, causing her to sigh in silence at the sensual movement. "No problem. That's where I was going to eat, since there's a flat screen and a table out there."

"The skating rink crew left, so it's just us now. Aren't you glad I stayed?"

Is that a trick question? She definitely was comfortable with him. Perhaps too comfortable, and that scared her. The last thing she needed to do was fall for a man with whom she knew a relationship was going to be out of the question. Blythe couldn't believe this was happening. She'd ignored his advances for a year, and now she actually thought she liked him after all. *What the hell is wrong with me?*

"Yes. I wasn't going to stay too much longer, though. The guy who owns the place is coming back at ten to lock up."

"No, I wasn't coming back at ten to lock up. You must've met Thomas, who manages the place."

"Oh…you own it?"

"I do as of two weeks ago. I decided to buy it instead of renting it so I can do whatever I want and have other events here, as well. When I saw it, I envisioned so many fun times for the children. Oh, and Broderick went in with me. He figured it would be a great investment as well."

She wasn't surprised that Tiffani's husband, who was one of Atlanta's wealthiest real estate moguls, had also purchased the building.

"Great idea."

"Yeah, the space is big enough for all kinds of events for the children. Linda has already scheduled a circus and a play group to come in the spring. I may rent it out, but for the most part I have first dibs, of course."

They painted for another hour, sometimes speaking briefly about the mural or the event. They'd made a lot of progress, and Blythe hated to admit that she was glad he'd stayed. His assistant arrived and informed them everything was set up in the lobby area. Blythe retreated to the ladies' room to wash her hands before meeting Preston. She was quite elated to see that the table was set up with a beautiful floral arrangement of different colored roses, china, wineglasses and cloth napkins. Preston was already there, sipping on water and changing the channel of the television with the remote.

"Oh, wow. You did all of this? For pizza?" Puzzled, she headed toward the table and was grateful he'd placed his sweater back on.

Standing, he walked around to the other chair

to pull it out. She sat and ran her fingers along the gold fork handle.

Preston settled back in his chair, facing her, and tucked his white napkin into his sweater. "I wanted something nice for you for all of your hard work with the project." He opened the box to display a yummy-looking pepperoni pizza. "There's also a salad."

"Oh, my. I don't know what to say. You didn't have to bring fine china. The roses are lovely."

"They're yours. I just wanted to say thank you for all of your work and dedication. You saw my vision and ran with it. It's like you're in my head. I appreciate it."

"You're very welcome, but it's not just me. You have a whole committee," she said, grabbing two slices of pizza and setting them on the antique-white plate with the gold band. She was used to eating pizza on a paper plate or a napkin, not an elegant plate, but she did appreciate the gesture.

"I'm throwing a thank-you party for everyone on New Year's Eve at Braxton's jazz club," he answered, taking a bite of his pizza.

"That sounds like fun." She nearly swooned as he licked his tongue to the side to capture a dab of the tomato sauce that had landed on the corner of his mouth. *What the hell is happening to me?* This man had never turned her on to this extent—but she'd never spent this much time with him, either.

"The invites should go out in a few days, I believe.

Linda handles all of that. You can bring a date if you want. Maybe the guy with the black truck."

Taking a sip of her soda, she pressed her lips together in a smile. "I'm not dating him."

"I know, but you said you were friends. You wouldn't want to hang with him on New Year's Eve? You have to kiss someone at midnight."

His mouth broke into the sexiest smile she'd ever seen on a man. The image of him placing his lips on hers jumped into her brain so fast, as if it was already there in her subconscious. Taking another sip of her drink, she glanced at the flat screen on the wall and checked her cell phone.

"Ha! Trust me. It won't be him or anyone else for that matter. The basketball game comes on soon." She needed to erase that image from her mind.

"I see you like sports, hence the cap, or do you like to watch the men in shorts sweating and running up and down the court, like my sister?"

"Well, that's part of the reason, but I do enjoy basketball. I can't get into football, but growing up, I would shoot hoops with my dad. He played in college." She was relieved at the subject change.

"Cool. I can't imagine you shooting hoops."

"I sucked at it, but my parents had three girls, no boys, and I was the only nongirlie one. Plus, I'm a daddy's girl, so if he wanted to play ball, we played ball. It was a way to exercise and stay active because, according to my mom, all I wanted to do was sit around and paint."

"She doesn't like the fact that you're an artist?"

"Mmm…now, I suppose, but growing up, no. I was an art major in college, but she wanted me to have a career that would make a lot of money such as business or finance, like my father. She said I'd be a starving artist, and for a time, I was—the first two years after college, until I got a job teaching art in a high school. I enjoyed it, but it wasn't my true calling. However, I did minor in business to please her, so I was able to parlay that knowledge into opening my studio."

"It seems to be doing very well."

"It is for now, but I know eventually the paint party craze will die down, so I sell my paintings at art shows and save my earnings for a rainy day. Trust me, it was no fun being a starving artist."

"Well, whenever you want to do a showing, let me know. You can have it here. I won't charge you."

"Thank you. I have some paintings that I'm putting some final touches on, but not enough for a huge showing yet."

They ate and watched basketball for a bit before heading back to finish the penguin mural. They were done two hours later, ahead of the time she'd anticipated if she'd painted alone.

"So, you aren't coming tomorrow?" he asked, walking her out to her car as he carried her roses and the box of leftover pizza.

Opening the passenger door, she stepped back as he placed the items on the floor mat. "No. It's the holiday season, which means more paint parties, and I have five tomorrow. I'll be back Wednesday evening. My receptionist is handling the one I was going to have that evening." She walked around to the driver's side with him close on her heels. Inside, the paint had drowned out his cologne, but now his scent tickled her nose once again, and she needed to hurry the heck up and speed off before she gave in to her emotions or whatever the hell she was feeling.

"That's fine. We have plenty of time. I have meetings tomorrow morning, and then I'm flying to New York City, but I'll be back Wednesday evening. If you need some help, I'll be happy to assist you."

Pivoting to face him, she ended up in his personal space, and her heartbeat raced. "I should be fine. You put me ahead of schedule by assisting tonight." *And I don't think I can handle any more alone time with you anytime soon.*

He stepped closer, and she hadn't even thought that was possible. She gasped as his strong hands encircled her waist and drew him toward her. He gave her an arrogant smirk.

"What?" he asked, puzzled. "I was just going to hug you."

"Oh…yes…of course." She laughed nervously and leaned in for the hug. The warmth of his body oozed right through his sweater, and she could feel his hard muscles. If she didn't move, she'd be a hot, steamy puddle at the man's feet.

Pulling back, he stared down at her. "What did

you think I was going to do? Kiss you?" he asked with an amused expression.

"Um…no. Well, maybe. I can never tell with you. You just surprised me. That's all."

"But you didn't push me away. I'm still holding you now, and you don't seem to mind."

"You're crazy." She shrugged with a slight laugh. "A hug from a friend is no big deal." She said it in a calm manner, but the butterflies in her stomach were fluttering rampantly.

"Mmm-hmm." He lowered his head, and his eyes darkened. "So, we're friends?"

She giggled and inwardly cursed herself for doing so. Schoolgirls giggled around their prospective crushes, and she was not a silly teenager whose crush was holding her as if he wasn't letting her go anytime soon. She shook off the fact that she was completely comfortable in his warm embrace. It was chilly out, but his body on hers had blocked out the cold air, and an electric heat dashed through her veins.

Staring up at Preston, Blythe gazed straight into his eyes, making sure she gave him full eye contact. She couldn't appear ruffled by being in his arms. It was just a friendly hug.

"You are my best friend's brother. And since I don't have any big brothers, you could be like one."

He chuckled, even though his facial expression was serious. A load of desire washed through her body as he lowered his lips to hers but didn't kiss her. Her breathing sped up as her chest rose and fell at what she knew in her heart he was going to do. Her lips parted by themselves, which resulted in another curse word in her head. The one she never spoke aloud in front of her parents.

"I don't want to be in the big brother category," he whispered.

Chapter 4

Preston had no idea what he was doing. This wasn't like him. Yes, he flirted with the breathtaking angel in his arms whenever he saw her because she was attractive and he enjoyed their light, fun banter. Plus, her laugh and smile were downright infectious, and he wanted to be the reason to make her smile. But now he was about to cross a line that he knew he wouldn't be able to step back over. What if Blythe slapped him? Pushed him away? Cursed him out? Not to mention Tiffani. Sure, his baby sister joked about hooking him up with Blythe because she was a good woman, but Tiffani would be devastated if he did anything to jeopardize their friendship.

However, those luscious lips were calling to him,

and her body against his was warm and alluring. She was nestled so close to him, he didn't know one from the other. They were almost one, and he decided to cross out the *almost*.

The first touch of his lips on hers was like a comforting mug of hot chocolate with whipped cream sprinkled with cinnamon on a cold day. The sweet, satisfied moan that erupted from her lips onto his caused him to delve deeper but slowly, circling her tongue with his in an erotic, forbidden dance. He stumbled with her back against the car, and he was pleased when her hand ran sensually up his cheek to his hair. She hadn't protested. Hadn't pushed him away. She met his kiss with the same fervor and vigor that he bestowed on her. He had to admit, he was rather surprised yet elated that she was so passionate. Just because she wanted to take things slow didn't make her a prude, but he wasn't expecting her to respond in the way that she was.

Their tempo sped up, and a sultry purr released from her as he became more ardent with his tongue and she relinquished the control of their kiss. He undid the scarf around her head and heard a few hairpins hit the car and the ground. He wove his hand through her thick, blown-out tresses and pulled her deeper into his mouth. Her lips against his were inviting, causing a rapid wave of pleasure to tremble through him.

In the back of his mind, something was screaming at him to stop. This wasn't right even though it felt like pure heaven. By now, if she was any other woman, he would've unzipped his pants, pulled down hers, wrapped her legs around his neck and sexed her right there on the hood of the car. But that wasn't going to happen, and not because she was his sister's best friend, even though he respected that. No, it was because he wanted her for more than just sex, and that scared the hell of out him.

When Blythe pulled away and wrestled out of his arms, her facial expression held regret. He stepped back and stared down at her, confused at her abruptness of cutting off their passionate kiss. He'd thought they were on the same page.

"Preston…we can't. This can't happen." Her voice trembled, and her eyes were rimmed with tears. "That was a big mistake."

"Blythe, I didn't mean to upset you." He reached out to caress her cheek, but she stepped away and opened the car door.

"I'm fine, but we can't do this if I'm going to help you on this project. I'm not one of your conquests that you can handle any way you want just because you're a man with money and power. I could give a rat's ass about that. Did you think the romantic dinner we had was going to get you into my panties? I'm not that kind of woman."

He stepped toward her but this time shoved his hands into his pockets. "I never said you were. I've never thought of you as a conquest, Blythe. I met you over a year ago. If I wanted you in that way, trust me, baby girl, I would've done everything in my power, as you say I have, to get you into my bed the same night we met—heck, or in your office after the paint party—but I didn't." He slid his hands out of his pockets and cupped her chin. "I wasn't ready for a woman like you. Not then. And for the record, I wasn't trying to have a romantic dinner. I simply wanted to thank you for your help and do something nice for you. Trust me, my imagination is quite vivid, and pizza on fine china and grocery-store-bought roses are far down my list of romantic things to do for a woman."

"Well…whatever. It can't happen again."

"Why not? What are you scared of? The way you responded to me wasn't as a woman afraid to let her guard down and do exactly what she wanted. You kissed me back with so much desire I nearly fell over."

"Prez, I honestly don't know what came over me." She slid into the driver's seat but didn't close the door. "This isn't like me at all."

He nodded because the truth was, he didn't know what had come over him, either, but it was something he wanted to explore. "Look, perhaps things got carried away." He stooped down in front of her. "However, I know women and I know me. That kiss signified that we're attracted to one another. I think we have been for a long while. We've never spent any time alone together until now."

She gave him one of her normal laugh-offs even

though he heard the nervousness in this one, unlike all the others.

"No…that's not it at all, and I think it's best that we just forget about it and continue working on the project for the children."

"Okay, we'll do it your way, but I don't think you're going to forget that toe-curling kiss anytime soon." Standing, he held on to the top of the opened door. "Good night, baby girl." He shut the door and stood back from the car as she backed out of the space and zoomed away from the parking lot.

Chuckling, Preston walked to his own car, thought about what had transpired between them and realized he wasn't going to forget that mesmerizing kiss anytime soon, either.

Preston was right and Blythe hated that. She'd tried like crazy to forget that mind-blowing kiss last night. Jogging on the treadmill, painting and a cold shower did nothing to erase it from her thought process. She could still feel the warmth of his lips and his hot tongue intertwined with hers. She couldn't believe she'd responded in the fashion that she had. Her head had screamed to stop, to push him away, but her heart had shouted for her to keep going at the top of its lungs. The man was superb with his hands and lips. She didn't expect anything less from him. But she wasn't expecting to enjoy it in the way she had, to the point of desiring more. And when the center of her core became heated with lust, she

had to pull back before she gave in to her awakening desires. Now she understood why he was one
of Atlanta's most sought-after bachelors. The man's
lips, which she'd always admired from a distance,
were a damn lethal weapon that should have been
outlawed. Plus, the emotion and passion behind his
kiss was knee-weakening, to say the least.

Sighing, she pulled out the paintbrushes that had
soaked overnight to be ready for her noon paint party
and placed them on paper towels to dry. She really
needed her usual morning bear claw to go with her
coffee, but that would require her to walk next door
to Tiffani's bakery. Blythe usually told her everything, but last night's kiss was one thing she wanted
to keep under wraps. When she'd arrived to work
that morning, she'd peeked into the bakery to find
Tiffani and her employees swamped with the morning rush. Blythe knew she couldn't avoid Tiffani all
day. They always found a way to chat during the
day, often right after the bakery's morning rush and
before the first paint session, which started at noon.

Once she finished setting up for her upcoming
session, Blythe headed to the lobby area, and her
eyes landed on the Christmas tree. The lights that
Preston had hung sparkled against the ornaments
that the art students had placed on it on Saturday.
Seeing the tree drew her thoughts right back to Preston's succulent lips on hers. His scent had lingered on
her clothes long after the kiss, and as soon as she'd
arrived home, she'd jumped right into the shower

to wash off the reminder. But it was no use. The water washed off the scent, but the memory of the woodsy, citrus fragrance still clogged her nostrils. The tender touch of his hands was still fresh and warm on her skin.

The light knock on the glass door yanked her from her thoughts and her stare rested on Tiffani, who carried a box and a cup of coffee. As always, she was perky, pretty and wearing a smile. Blythe mustered up one as well, and hoped she didn't blurt out that she'd kissed Preston. If he'd been some other guy, that's exactly what would have happened. She had to stay focused so that it wouldn't spill out of her mouth.

Unlocking the door, she stepped back for Tiffani to enter. "Hey, girl."

"Hey, *chica.* I decided to bring you some goodies. I was surprised I didn't see you this morning when I opened."

Blythe closed and locked the door and followed Tiffani to the seating area. "Yeah, I needed to set up for my paint sessions today. I have one at noon and another starting at twelve thirty, so I'll be shooting back and forth between rooms."

"Well, I figured you'd be busy. So, how is my brother's project coming along? I'm so happy you volunteered to help."

Dang it. Why is Preston the first topic after all? Blythe sipped her coffee, bit into a bear claw and dabbed her mouth with a napkin. She'd hoped they would discuss everything but the project. All it did was remind her that she would have to see Preston again soon.

"Everything is coming along. Devin's team pretty much built the set yesterday, and I did the penguin mural I was telling you about."

"Oh, good. I spoke to Preston briefly yesterday. He's expecting one hundred fifty to two hundred kids."

"You better get started on those cupcakes now, girl," Blythe teased.

"I know, right? With those and all of the Christmas orders, I have a lot on my plate, but it's worth it."

"Well, so much has happened in your life this past year."

Tiffani beamed with delight. "Yes, indeed. I married a caring, loving man. He's so wonderful to me and KJ that it's surreal. Sometimes I literally have to pinch myself in the mornings when I wake up and see Broderick's handsome face next to me. Sometimes he's already awake, just staring at me with this peaceful expression."

"Well, I'm glad you found the man of your dreams who treats you with the respect you deserve."

Tiffani's late husband and her son's father had been verbally and emotionally abusive during their marriage, causing Tiffani to vow never to marry again. However, meeting Broderick Hollingsworth changed her mind. He truly was a genuine man who loved Tiffani and her son dearly. Blythe was ecstatic for Tiffani when she married Broderick in a beautiful beach ceremony on his private island in the Florida Keys.

"Me, too," Tiffani stated with a bright smile. "So what about you? Did Michael ever call you back?"

Blythe frowned, trying to remember who the heck that was. Preston's kiss had washed out all other names, and her mind drew a blank. But eventually she did remember her third and last date with the engineer and his eight hands.

"No, and I don't want him to. I told you that man turned into a squid after one good-night smooch that wasn't even all that. I doubt he'll call and I don't want him to. As usual wanting to take things slow has its drawbacks"

"Yeah, but that just means those men aren't for you if they can't wait until you're ready. Men should respect you and your decision."

"I agree. I just want to know a man before I jump into bed with him. I'm not necessarily waiting until marriage, but I want to know he's the one I'm going to marry or, at the very least, be in a long-term committed, monogamous relationship with."

"I hear you, Blythe. I wish my brother thought like that. I mean, don't get me wrong, he's a wonderful, caring man like our father and my husband. And I know Prez isn't having sex with all the women he's dating, but I just want him to settle down with one. A good one who believes in him. He's getting too old for his player ways. Plus, Mom keeps nagging him that he needs to find a good woman and stop dating gold digging thots. Yes, my mother actually said *thots*."

"Oh, my goodness. You know your mom swears she's our age. But as far as Preston, perhaps he'll turn over a new leaf. Or maybe he just hasn't found the one yet." *Not that I'm implying it's me, because it's not.*

"Yeah… I suppose you're right." Tiffani shrugged, biting into her blueberry muffin. "I just want him in a healthy relationship. A lot of women seek him out because of his wealth."

"Is he dating anyone serious right now?" Blythe probed, trying to keep her tone in the same light-hearted, I-really-don't-care manner. But she did care. The way he'd kissed her as if she belonged to him had shaken her, and a part of her almost wished it was true.

"Who knows? According to him, he doesn't have a girlfriend, just female friends. The one he brought to Thanksgiving dinner probably won't be the one at my Christmas party, and the one at the New Year's Eve party at Braxton's club will be someone he met the day before. After a while their faces and names become blurry in my memory, and his, too, more than likely."

Blythe chuckled. That point just solidified why she definitely could not fall for Preston. So what, he'd kissed her? So what, it was the best first kiss ever? So what, according to him she'd never for-get it? He was just being arrogant and overly confident. *No, wait. I'm still thinking about it.* However, none of that meant they should go further, even if his comment still sounded loud in her ears: *"I wasn't ready for a woman like you. Not then."* Was he implying that now he was ready for a woman like her, or ready for *her*?

"Well, I'm sure whomever your brother settles down with, she'll have to be someone special to get the president of the player's club to fall."

Standing, Tiffani swiped her cell phone and mug from the coffee table. "Most definitely. Gotta run. I have to bake some sweet treats for an order but just wanted to stop by for our morning chat."

After Tiffani left, Blythe breathed easy again. She hated not telling her friend what happened. She had always confided in her. Though there really wasn't anything to tell. It was just one kiss, and nothing was going to progress from it. She didn't want to be just one of many women Preston had on rotation. And she didn't want to get Tiffani's hopes up.

A beep from her cell phone jerked her from her thoughts. Sliding it off the table, she opened it to several pictures of Hope from Preston. Smiling, she scrolled through the pictures, and her heart stopped beating at the last one. It was a selfie of Preston and Hope lying on the floor together. The dog was adorable with her paws up, but her master's smile was exquisite and sexy as if it was just for her.

"Hey, Blythe."

Startled, she looked up to see Ms. Bernice walking in and taking her jacket off.

"Sure is chilly this morning, but it's supposed to warm up this weekend. Taking my granddaughters to see the Christmas decorations at the Atlanta Botanical Garden on Sunday." The older lady paused and eyed Blythe carefully. "Are you okay?" She continued to her desk and placed her coat on the back of her chair before walking back over to the seating area. "Something happened?" she inquired with a concerned expression.

Blythe turned the phone all the way off when she noticed Ms. Bernice straining to see what was on the screen. "No, I'm fine," she answered, standing. "Just thinking about our busy week, but that's a good thing. I can pay the bills and your paychecks," she teased, realizing she was too giddy. That wasn't her at all. She made an effort to regain her calm.

"How's the Winter Wonderland project going?"

"So far so good. Going back tomorrow after work."

Ms. Bernice nodded. "Good. I'm glad you decided to help. I thought you'd be tired today, but you look refreshed and glowing."

"Well, you know I love volunteering when needed, especially for a good cause. I have an hour before my paint party, so I'm going to head back to my office to finish payroll."

Blythe scurried off to her office, closed the door and sank into the love seat. She'd finished payroll already, but she had to get away from the conversation before everything that happened last night spilled from her mouth. Ms. Bernice was very observant, and if she said Blythe was glowing then she was. Usually the effects of a first kiss didn't last this long. In fact, first kisses informed her whether or not there would be a second. Unfortunately, this time there wasn't going to be a second, even though the kiss said differently. *Is it too early for a glass of wine?*

Blythe pulled up to the event venue the next evening, relieved not to see Preston's Aston Martin or his Range Rover. The skating rink was complete, minus the ice. The spot where the Ferris wheel would reside was roped off. Upon the entering the building, she was greeted by Hope as she charged toward her, wagging her tail affectionately. Stooping down, she rubbed the dog's head and glanced around for her owner, but they were alone in the lobby. The double doors to the main hall were closed, and Blythe could hear electric saws, hammering and the voices of the men from Devin's crew. It was five o'clock so they would probably leave soon. Trekking to the doors, she peered through the window of one of the doors and saw Preston chatting with Jonathan Dexter, Supreme Construction's head builder. Santa's Village seemed to be complete, and the Christmas trees surrounding it were beautifully decorated in an array of colors. As if he sensed her staring in his direction, Preston turned his head slowly and released a sexy smile that sent a rush of goose bumps along her skin. He motioned for her to come in and mouthed for her to leave Hope in the lobby.

Sighing, Blythe petted the dog once more and hoped that her owner would leave with the rest of the crew. Stepping inside, she was surprised to see all of the progress that had been made in the short time frame that she'd been away.

"Wow! It's gorgeous. This is definitely Santa's Village," she said, trying to keep her eyes off Preston and instead perusing the scenery. Plush red carpet led to a platform where a huge red-and-gold throne sat waiting for Mr. Claus. The mechanical animals and people, Christmas trees and Nativity scene sat on the fake snow, just as she'd sketched out. She walked along the carpet covered with plastic as the men followed behind.

"The sled and the petting area for the reindeer and other live animals will be behind the stage. That's the only part of the village that isn't complete," Jonathan stated. "Well, that and the murals at the entrance, but that's why you're here."

"Exactly." She turned toward Preston. "I see you're back in town, Prez." She was relieved it came out in a regular tone even though on the inside she was filled with jitters as if she'd drunk five cups of strong black coffee with sugar.

"Yep. Hope and I just arrived from New York, and I instructed my driver to bring me straight here. I wanted to see the progress in person. Plus, I wasn't sure if you needed any help again this evening. I enjoyed painting with you." His lips formed the last comment, but the wicked twinkle in his eyes said, *I enjoyed kissing you.*

Blythe was disappointed when Jonathan excused himself and she was left alone with Preston. "Actually, no. I'm staying only a few hours. Just long enough to complete the entrance. Mandi is coming back with me on Sunday to do the ski scene." That was one big fat lie, but she couldn't have him stay. She was trying her hardest to stay composed.

He nodded as he glanced at her lips and then back at her eyes as if he'd been caught. "Cool. Well, Hope is here if you need her to pose. I wasn't sure if you'd received the pictures or not. I never heard back."

"Oh...yeah. I got them and sketched out a cute scene with her and some children having a snowball fight." She opened her tote bag, withdrew her sketch pad and turned to the page before handing it to him. "Here you go."

He examined the scenes, nodding his head in a pleased manner. "This looks just like my Hope. I wasn't sure when I hadn't heard back from you whether or not you were avoiding me." He shut the sketch pad and handed it back to her.

Stifling a gulp, she stared up at him and prayed he wouldn't be able to read into her upcoming lie. "I'm not avoiding you. Why would I?"

"Um...because of what happened between us the other night. *The kiss.*"

She laughed as if it was no big deal, even though the simple mention of it set her heart ablaze. "Oh, that? I'm fine. Haven't even thought about it."

He raised a curious eyebrow as if he didn't believe her. "Wow…well, I've certainly thought about it and you." He stepped closer, and his eyes darkened. "*A lot.* That was some kiss, baby girl. I can't stop thinking about you."

Releasing a wicked smile, she patted his cheek softly. "Well, I've always been told I was a good kisser. Now, if you'll excuse me, I need to get started with the mural of your precious pup. Talk to you later," she said in cheery, nonchalant tone and pivoted on her heel to jet back down the red carpet before her face turned scarlet from the heat rising in her cheeks.

While she worked on the mural, Blythe noticed he was still there, strolling the venue with Linda, who seemed to be jotting down notes of things he was pointing out. After a while, the tree decorators returned to finish the trees and hang fresh evergreen garland intertwined with frosted pine cones and silver ornaments around the ceiling. She was grateful that this evening she wouldn't be alone with Preston. Being so close to him earlier, and the fact that he seemed serious when he said he couldn't stop thinking about her, had caused her once again to question what the heck was happening between them. She'd managed to keep him at bay for now, but Preston wasn't the kind of man to let sleeping dogs lie. Eventually he'd either flirt or, worse, kiss her even more profoundly than before so she could never say again she hadn't thought about the kiss.

Two hours later, she was exhausted and done for the evening. She decided she'd come back in the morning since her first paint party didn't start until two o'clock. Preston and Linda had disappeared through the entrance doors around an hour ago, and she'd assumed he'd left. She was surprised he hadn't bid her goodbye, but she figured his male ego was slightly damaged since she'd acted as if their kiss meant nothing to her. The truth was far from it, but she couldn't get involved with a man like him. She'd left her days of dating the party playboy type in her early twenties. No point in wasting any more of her precious time on relationships that weren't going anywhere.

The tree decorators were still there when she finished cleaning up and packing her supplies away. She waved goodbye to Jonathan, who was overseeing the assembly of the game stations. Pushing the door to the lobby open, she nearly jumped out of her skin when Hope ran to her, and her eyes caught the gaze of Preston sitting on the couch. He was working on his laptop as the sports channel played in the background. "You're still here?" Her heart restricted in her chest. *Is he waiting for me?*

"Yeah, waiting for my driver to return. He dropped us off here from the private airfield and then left to take my luggage to my house, but there's a bad accident on 285 and he's stuck in traffic. I'd take a cab or MARTA but they don't allow dogs. Neither does Uber. I just checked."

"Oh..." She halted as the words on the tip of her tongue almost spilled out. He lived on her way home, but that would mean she'd be alone with him in her car. That was too close, too soon.

"I'm fine, but Hope hasn't eaten since we left New York, and it's past her dinnertime. I hadn't planned on being here this long."

"I have some baby carrots in my bag. Can she have those while you wait for your driver to return? Misty ate them all the time."

"Yes. She eats those and apple slices for treats. Thank you."

She reached into her tote bag, which contained the fruit and raw veggies she usually snacked on to avoid eating junk food. Sitting on the floor with Hope, she held out her hand with a couple of carrots, and the dog immediately snatched them and chomped them down.

Sighing, Blythe knew she was going to regret her decision later. "Prez, I can take you and Hope home. It's on my way." She noticed that Hope had on her car harness vest.

"Thank you for the offer. Let me call and see where my driver is."

Preston placed the call while she continued feeding Hope carrots, eavesdropping on the conversation at the same time. She kind of hoped the driver was only five minutes away. But she knew that wasn't the case when she heard Preston say that the driver was at least an hour away. Apparently the direction they would travel in would be smooth sailing. Preston told the driver he had a ride and instructed him to go home to his family.

With that confirmation, Blythe put on a smile and told herself to stay calm and strong. At most, it would be a thirty-minute drive. She'd drop them off at the gate and then head to her own home, where she'd once again have to take a cold shower or paint out her sexual frustrations.

Chapter 5

Once they were on the road, Blythe racked her brain for safe topics to discuss. Luckily, Preston fiddled with his cell phone, and she hoped he would continue to do so all the way to his home. A slew of beeps from the phone had sounded when he'd entered the car. He was smiling quite hard, so perhaps he was gearing up for a hot date that night. The thought sank her heart, and she silently reprimanded herself for caring. That stupid kiss had her thinking crazy, and she needed to stop. The man clearly had other women on his mind. *And see, that is the very reason I can never take him seriously.*

He shut the phone off and glanced in her direction as they crossed the bridge over the interstate. The other side of 285 was indeed backed up, but the side she prepared to turn onto ran smoothly. If she drove fast enough, she'd have Preston home in twenty minutes instead of thirty. However, they were stuck at the red light, and the silence between them had become uncomfortable, especially since he kept staring at her as if he wanted to say something. Perhaps he was searching for safe topics, as well.

"Hot date tonight?" she asked, breaking the unbearable silence. *What happened to the safe topics?*

He gave her a sexy grin. "No. Had some offers, of course…but not interested. My focus is elsewhere."

Her racing pulse settled back to normal. "Oh, well, you were cheesing mighty hard a moment ago," she teased him.

"I see you were paying attention to me. Mmm-hmm. Interesting. But no, it was one of my business partners I met with in New York."

"So, how was the trip?" she asked, merging onto the interstate and glad they'd moved on to something else.

"Fantastic. I attended a tech show to introduce the upcoming arcade game models I created for next year."

"I didn't know you did those, too."

"I do it *all*, baby girl."

I'll bet you do. "Mmm…so, I noticed you have vintage games at your home. When I was working with Devin and Sasha on the design plans, I had to fight the urge to go play *Ms. Pac-Man*. That was my favorite game back in the day, along with *Donkey Kong*."

"You could've played it. They all work. Linda informed me earlier that a new game I ordered arrived while I was away and is already set up. I'm excited to go home and try it out."

"What is it?"

"It's called *Cruis'n Exotica*. It's a racing game."

"Oh, I love those, too. I think that's how I learned how to drive."

"Me, too. You should come up and check it out. It needs two drivers. Can't play alone."

She glanced at him out of the corner of her eye. When his voice deepened seductively, goose bumps began to caress her skin. She tapped the steering wheel lightly, hoping to reduce the warmth that radiated over her.

"I'm sure you can. You place the other side on auto. I'm familiar with racing games, Mr. Chase."

"Mmm…but two people *are* so much better, beautiful. You don't want to play with me?

"Prez…" She pressed down a moan in her throat as her insides started to burn again with desire for him. The man was unraveling her with every passing second, and they were only discussing video games. *Is no topic safe with him?* That kiss wasn't *that* damn good, for her to be having these kinds of sensations and withdrawal symptoms. No, wait, she was only fooling herself with that nonsense. That kiss had kept her up at night, trying to memorize every single detail of it. And she had. She remembered the beginning, the middle and the end of it.

"What? I'm not flirting. I'm serious, Blythe."

"I'll think about it. What else did you do in New York?" *Wait. That topic may not be safe, either. Tiffani did say he had female friends in most of the cities he visited.*

"Braxton's second jazz club finally opened, so I hung out with him and Elle for a bit. Elle had a fashion show for her winter wedding attire collection. I hadn't planned on going to that, but she insisted. Saw some tuxedos I liked and ended up ordering them."

"I just love her wedding gowns. They're gorgeous. I heard they're expecting. I'm happy for them."

"Yeah, me, too. I'm glad, considering why they weren't together for ten years."

"Wow, so he really didn't show up for the wedding? I'm sure Elle was crushed. I couldn't imagine being left at the altar."

"Yeah, she was pretty inconsolable. My other cousin Cannon and I tried to talk some sense into Brax, but he just couldn't go through with it. He wasn't ready, but now they're married and happy. They're soul mates. Get off at the upcoming exit," he suggested. "There's a shortcut that I use. Shaves off about seven minutes, and sometimes my exit is backed up during this time of day."

"No problem." *The quicker the better,* she thought before she took him up on his offer. The side of her that still reminisced about the kiss wanted to play; however, she didn't know if she could handle being alone with him anymore.

"So, are you going to play the racing game with me?"

Dang it. She'd hoped he was teasing or had forgotten. "Um…don't you have plenty of girls on rotation? I'm sure they would love to play with you," she joked, veering toward the exit.

He chuckled. "Turn right at the light, and no, I prefer to play with the *woman* seated next to me."

"Preston…"

"I promise not to flirt."

"Mmm-hmm." She turned right and recognized the intersection. "You've been flirting for the past ten minutes."

"Seriously, I would love for you to play the racing game with me, and Hope wants you to come, too." He glanced at the sleeping dog stretched out in the backseat. "Don't you, girl?"

"She's been snoring for the past twenty minutes, but fine. Besides, I'm curious about the game." *What the heck did I just say?*

Twenty minutes later, she found herself in the game room playing *Ms. Pac-Man* while waiting for Preston, who was preparing Hope's food. Blythe couldn't believe she'd agreed to come up, but a part of her needed to prove to herself that whatever she thought she felt for Preston wasn't real and that she could be comfortable around him.

"I see you went straight to *Ms. Pac-Man*," he said, entering the room and setting some platters of food on a table in the bar area. "My personal chef stopped by earlier and left dinner in the fridge. Do you like Thai food? It's curried cashew chicken with carrots and brown rice."

"I do, but don't prolong the beating you're about to receive in the racing game. I always win." *Wait. Did I just challenge a gamer?*

"Uh-huh. You do know what I do for a living, right? Plus, I know it may not seem like it, but I'm a techie nerd at heart. A true gamer. I will win. I will destroy you, so buckle up, baby girl."

"Ha!" She walked over to the racing game. "What side do you want?"

Joining her, he waved his hand in front of it. "I'm a gentleman. I'll let you pick."

She slid into the right side, and he followed suit on the left. He scooted his seat back a tad to accommodate his long legs. His right leg brushed her left one, and she wasn't sure if it was on purpose or not, but when she glanced at him, he winked and moved it.

"Are you ready?" she asked. *Because I'm not.*

"Born ready. It's about to be on." He revved the accelerator and placed his hands on the steering wheel.

She revved her side louder. "Prepare to eat my dust."

"Oh, you want to make a small wager on that?"

"I'm sure your idea of a small wager is what I make in a year. No, thank you."

"No, baby girl." His voice deepened as a sly smile emerged. "Not money."

Stifling a gulp, she cleared her throat. "Then what?" she inquired curiously as he scooted closer to her, ran his finger gently down her cheek and landed it on her lips. The subtle touch on her skin elicited emotions she couldn't explain and reminded her of why she shouldn't have come.

"Well? What do you want?" she questioned, regretting it as soon as she asked.

His lips curled into a naughty, *How the Grinch Stole Christmas* grin.

"One more kiss."

As soon as he spoke his thoughts, Preston knew he had to be victorious. At first he'd considered letting Blythe win, until she started to challenge him and he realized she was dead serious. But wasn't she aware that gaming was his life? He played online with other gamers who didn't know he was the founder of JP3 Chase Technologies, the creator of half of the latest popular games on the market. They knew him only as The Chaser.

When Blythe had first entered the Winter Wonderland venue earlier, he'd wanted to strip her of her painter's jumpsuit, pull off the hair scarf and devour her right there. The past few days since their kiss had been thought-provoking and awakening, to say the least. His mind had raced with all kinds of amorous thoughts about them, and he found himself wanting to know so much more about her. But he needed to kiss her once more. He needed to make sure it wasn't a phase he was going through because it was the holidays, and he was in a sentimental mood.

Women didn't stay on his mind like this. He'd never thought about a woman when he was in his element, but Blythe and the kiss were in the forefront of his brain during the technology conference. Even when he was at Braxton's club or at Elle's fashion show, not a single woman piqued his interest. They were downright beautiful women and normally he would've flirted with them all, taken the sexiest one back to his hotel room at the Waldorf Astoria and had hot sex all night. Instead he ignored them all, went back to his hotel, ordered a romantic comedy movie and thought about Blythe all night. He knew this woman was different than the rest when he watched a romantic comedy and enjoyed it.

Stopping by the venue tonight wasn't on his agenda, but he knew she would be there and he had to see her again. His private jet couldn't land fast enough. He had to make sure he wasn't going crazy for her, but when he witnessed her affectionately feeding carrots to his dog, he knew this woman was special.

Preston rested his eyes on her face. She was speechless, to say the least, but he was glad she hadn't darted out of there, either. But when a sly smile emerged as if she was up for the challenge, he realized maybe he had her pegged wrong. Maybe she really could play and play well. Or maybe, like him, she needed to sort out her feelings and wanted to kiss him again. He hoped it was the latter.

"Fine, and if I win, you can never flirt with me again," she stated seriously.

That was a promise he knew he couldn't keep. "Then don't look so damn scrumptious and adorable in front of me, baby girl."

"Whatever. Let's get this race going."

After agreeing on the course in Thailand to go with their cuisine for the evening, they started the race. He had to stay focused and concentrate on the task at hand, for winning the game meant so much more than earning the higher score. He had to admit, while she wasn't a pro like him, she could keep up and was quite competitive. She was on his tail and had even jetted in front of him at one point, but he zoomed past and she swerved, causing her to crash into the wall and blow up her last car. She screamed out "No!" and jumped up and ran as if she was actually running away from the burning car.

He chuckled. "You're hilarious, woman."

Leaning against the pool table, she laughed un-controllably. "Dang it… I just lost."

"Not entirely. I mean, kissing me again is defi-nitely not a loss."

She stopped laughing, and a serious expression reached her face as if she'd forgotten they'd made a bet.

"You mean…like this second? Can we eat first?" she questioned, glancing over at the food. "We don't want a cold dinner."

"I have a microwave behind the bar."

Pursing her lips together, she grasped the edge of the pool table. "That's right. You did win."

"I always do, baby girl."

Blythe couldn't believe this was happening. Again. She couldn't believe she'd made a bet, and a nonsensical bet at that, with a gamer. Sure, she'd won video games the majority of the time before, but usually she was playing against the computer, not an actual person who just so happened to invent video games for a living. She grasped the pool table harder, and her breath lodged in her lungs as she waited for his next move. He was still seated but held her eyes in his smoldering gaze, and she couldn't tear them away. However, he just sat there. Had he changed his mind? Was he messing with her? Why was he pro-longing it? He was the one who had suggested one more kiss, and for some damn reason, she'd agreed.

Now she just wanted to get it over with so she could breathe again.

"Changed your mind?" she asked. "Scared you won't forget it? Scared it's going to keep you up at night?" *Like the last one did to me, tossing and turning with insomnia?*

A sinfully sexy grin inched up his jaw as he let out a wicked snicker. "Why are you way over there? I would say you're the scared one."

"I'm not scared of kissing you again. I wouldn't have agreed to the bet if I was." She strolled back over with lead legs weighing her down like an anchor and tingles seared across her skin. "Just like last time, it's not going to mean anything." She slid back into her seat and turned her body toward him. "Go ahead. Lay it on me and then we can dive into the Thai food. I'm starving."

Preston didn't answer but instead yanked her to him and scooped her up so that he cradled her in his arms. His intense stare returned as he brushed his lips on hers. His touch was light. Tender and sweet. For a moment she thought that was all he was going to do and was about to release a sigh of relief, but his tongue sought hers and circled around it. The kiss was deep and slow. *Arousing* wasn't even the word as he delved into her mouth more profoundly with each passing second. This kiss was different than before. It was more passionate and heat-filled than the last one, and she hadn't thought that was possible. But this time it was as if she'd missed him and needed to be wrapped in his embrace.

A disappointed shiver rushed over her when he pulled back. His mouth lingered over hers while his eyes were intoxicated with lust. Was he stopping? She sure hoped not as she deepened her tongue into his mouth, which released a pleased groan and a half smile from him. She couldn't get enough of his tantalizing tongue looping with hers in a kiss that shot electric bolts from the roots of her hair down to her red-painted toenails.

Lifting her body up but not leaving his dangerous mouth, Blythe straddled his lap and wrapped her hands around his neck. His hands settled on her hips, pulling her even closer to him as the welcomed assault on her lips never ended. The erotic sounds that arose from her throat were startling and out of character. When his lips left hers, she was about to yell out no, but he placed them on the side of her neck, which awakened more unfamiliar moans. Clenching his shoulders, she leaned her head back as he nibbled on and licked her skin with fast, fervent strokes. He wasn't letting up anytime soon, it seemed, and that was fine with her. The blissful passion that erupted in her settled at her center. She tried to compress the tingles by shifting on his lap, but that only made the hardness of him pulse through his pants.

"This isn't part of the bet," she whispered.

"Do you want me stop?" he asked, resting his eyes on hers.

His question shocked her. "No, I'm fine."

"Tell me when you need me to and I will."

"Okay."

He continued trailing kisses on her skin, and she surprised herself by not stopping him, but she trusted his sincerity. Some of the men she'd gone out with would do everything in their power to make her go all the way. But this time, if she wasn't careful, she was going to make the decision herself. And she had a feeling she wouldn't regret it. That scared her. She was supposed to have willpower, but now being with Preston was breaking down the barrier as no other man had been able.

"Um…" She tapped his shoulder.

"Now?" He slid his hands from her butt and rested them on her waist.

"No, it's just cramped in here. My back is push-ing into the steering wheel."

"Hold on to me."

After she wrapped her arms around his neck, he slid out of the game and slammed his lips on hers once more as he carried her to the sectional leather couch and laid her down on it with him following on top of her.

"Better?" he asked, hovering his lips over hers.

"Yes."

He captured her lips again and sank in deeper,

showing no mercy. He rested his hands on either side of her face, and she was almost disappointed they weren't roaming over her body. However, she was grateful he was being respectful. She ran her hand up to his hair and wove it into his lush, dark, silky curls. A guttural groan rushed from him, and he jerked up and stared at her with dark, heated eyes.

"You're beautiful."

"Thank you, Prez. You're not so bad yourself, handsome."

She reached her lips up to meet his, but he breathed out as a strained expression crossed his features, and he shifted slightly on her. That's when she felt him hard against her center. She gulped as he cupped her face and trembled against her body.

Blythe cracked a smile. Maybe she wasn't the one having an issue. She was used to having willpower, even though Preston was chipping away at it. "Are you okay?"

"Yeah. I…um…may need to stop before I begin to want something I can't have, and I respect you too much even to ask."

"I appreciate that. Thank you. Most men would try to coax me or convince me otherwise."

He slid off her and sat up on the couch, facing her. Titling her head, she stared at him in disbelief.

"I'm not a perv."

"No. I wouldn't be here if I thought you were. It's

just… I…" She stopped. Was she really about to be honest with him?

"Truth moment. It's something my parents would say to me and Tiff growing up. So, truth moment. What do you want to tell me?"

She knew about the truth moments. She'd heard Tiffani say it to her son when she knew he wasn't being honest about something and needed to confess.

Clearing the frog from her throat, she decided to come clean. After all, they were adults, and game time was over. "I'm very comfortable with you, and I'm surprised. That's all."

"I'm glad you are, Blythe. I've always admired you from a distance, and I have to say, I've enjoyed the time we've spent together lately, getting to know each other."

"Me, too."

"So, how do you feel about us continuing on this path? I promise, no pressure, but I…I like you, a lot. I'd love to see where this could go. Tiffani has joked to me about hooking us up since we met. My sister knows me well, and I think she feels that we would be good together. I've always trusted her judgment."

Blythe couldn't believe they were having this conversation. She'd kept him at bay and out of her thoughts because of his playboy ways. However, here she was contemplating exploring more with him, and the fact that they'd just had another mind-blowing kissing session wasn't helping her clouded mind at the moment.

"I didn't think you were the dating type. It always seemed as if you've had a different woman on your arm every other week."

"I am, but sometimes the women I go out with turn out to be what I would consider not the dating type. Some of them only want to date me because of who I am, or rather who they think I am. I'm not going to lie to you and say that I haven't had my share of one-night stands, friends-with-benefits or women-of-the-month, as Tiffani likes to say. But after a while that gets old, and hell, so am I. Yes, when I first met you, I was in awe of everything about you and laid on the charm. There was something about you that I knew I would have to commit to. I told you before I wasn't ready for a woman like you. But spending these last few days with you has woken me up, and I'd like to explore where this could lead. There's something between us. We can go as slow as you want, and if it doesn't work out, we could still be friends."

Blythe soaked in everything he said, and in her heart she knew he was sincere. When she'd first met him, she was very much attracted to him as well, but because of his rep, she hadn't wanted to go down that road with him.

"I'd like that, but for now, let's keep this between

us just in case we realize that kissing is the only thing we have in common."

"Perfect, and just so you know, I'm not seeing anyone at the moment or juggling a slew of women, in case you were concerned about that."

"I wasn't, but now that you mention it…didn't you have a hot date that night when you carried the tree inside for me?" she reminded him with a questioning smirk.

"I did and I canceled it. I ended up going to KJ's karate tournament. I don't like missing those. And are you seeing anyone?"

"Uh…no. Unless you count you, then no."

"I count." Standing, he grabbed her hand. "Let's get something to eat."

"Can we eat on the chaise lounges by the fireplace? They're so comfortable."

"No problem. I spend a lot of time there…staring at your painting and lately thinking more about the breathtaking artist."

She stood on her tippy toes and kissed him lightly on the lips. "Didn't I tell you my kisses are unforgettable?"

"That you did," he replied, kissing her forehead.

Once they were settled with their food, Blythe was in such a daze she could barely concentrate on eating the delicious food. The turn of events happened so fast, but in a way, their light, fun back-and-forth banter over the past year had set them up for the moment they were experiencing now. She caught his eyes on her and an expression that told her he wanted to ask her something.

"What?"

"Tell me, why did you decide to take a dating break? I know you said it had nothing to do with a broken heart, but I'm just curious, if you don't mind."

Taking a sip of her lemonade, she dabbed the side of her mouth with a napkin. "I don't mind. No, it wasn't over a broken heart even though my ex, who I thought I would eventually marry, cheated on me pretty much the entire time we were together. Honestly, at first it didn't start out as a break. It was more of a drought. I was busy opening my business, and dating became secondary. I just didn't have time. I've never really cared for casual sex or one-night stands. Don't get me wrong—I've had the friends-with-benefits situations, and I'm not a holier-than-thou prude by any means. It's just been more of a spiritual awakening for me. Getting to know Blythe Rose Ventura better. I still date, but I'd rather learn more about the person and have a soul connection before a body connection. I don't have a ballpark figure of how long that will be, but I would prefer to be in an actual relationship before having sex. It just baffles me how some men really think we're having sex after two dates."

"So, you're not celibate or anything like that?"

"No, but I would like to be in a relationship that

would lead to marriage. That's the end game. I want a husband and children someday. I want to be in sync in mind, body, spirit and soul. Sex is so much more than just physical…or at least, it is to me. I want a complete connection before I just jump in the bed with someone. Trust me, I've been there, and it wasn't satisfying, special or loving at all."

"So tell me about the ex who gave you the wake-up call."

"We were together for two years. Off and on. My friends told me about his reputation, but I ignored them. Of course, he was a player, but I thought I could change him because I'm a good woman. Why would he ever play around on me? He laid on the charm and I believed him. Besides, he was handsome, was educated, had a very lucrative career and was very close with his family. And over thirty. Most men over thirty are ready to settle down. Playing games should be over with. He was the first to bring up marriage, not me. I even met his mother after only a month of dating him. After some time, I started to see the red flags, but I ignored them as he reassured me he wasn't seeing anyone else. Well, my wake-up call was when I caught him in bed with two women. I wasn't heartbroken, just pissed at myself for not seeing the signs all along."

"Wow. I'm sorry. You don't have to worry about me trying to get you in my bed. If we get to that point, it's your decision."

"Thank—" She stopped and laughed as Hope interrupted their conversation by bouncing up on the chaise lounge with Blythe and snuggling at her feet. She leaned over and rubbed the dog's back.

"That's her spot when she's ready to go to sleep for the night," Preston explained, setting his plate on the coffee table between them and sliding over to sit next to Hope. She rested her head on his lap, wagged her tail and went back to sleep.

Standing, Blythe stretched her arms out and yawned. "It's late, and I have to be up early in the morning. I'm going to finish Hope's mural before going to work."

Preston stood, grabbed her hands and kissed them softly. "Don't overexert yourself. We have plenty of time before Christmas Eve."

"I know, but after a while I won't have time because of the busy season. The closer to Christmas, the more booked Paint, Sip, Chat is."

"Well, I appreciate all the help. Hope and I are going to the hospital on Friday afternoon. Do you have a session?"

"I'm free after two. I was going to use that time to get some work done on the Winter Wonderland project, but I can come for a bit. I'd love to meet the children you care so much about."

"Perfect. They're having a read-a-thon for the younger ones. I'm giving them all tablets filled with tons of children's books and educational games. I'm also sending hard copies of the books to their homes. It would be too many to bring to the hospital, but I'm going to read a couple of books during story time. Maybe you can, too."

"I'd love to."

She headed to the elevator with him striding next to her. A relaxed, protected feeling washed over Blythe when he pulled her close to him and kissed her gently on the lips, followed by a sweet kiss on the forehead.

"For the record, that clown didn't know what he had. You're a precious gem, Blythe, and I promise we will take things as slow as you want. You're the kind of woman I don't want to hurt or do anything to push away."

"I appreciate that, and thank you for a wonderful time. I enjoyed the racing game. I almost want to play again," she teased.

"One more time. I'll even show you the secrets on how to win."

She dropped her purse to the floor. "Game on."

Chapter 6

Blythe unbraided her hair in the mirror that hung on the inside of her closet door in her office. She'd washed and dyed her tresses with a brown rinse the night before. She'd braided her hair and then set it with huge twist rollers. The ringlets of curls and the color had come out as beautifully as she'd hoped. Shaking it, she fixed a few strands before applying a light coat of red lip gloss and eyeliner. Blythe couldn't believe she was stressing over seeing Preston. She usually never got riled up over preparing to see whoever she was dating, even though what they were doing wasn't dating. In fact, they'd never been on an actual date, but in a way, it wasn't necessary. She'd enjoyed getting to know him better without the pressure of stating they were dating or in a relationship. This way was more organic and carefree without the nonsense of titles. She looked forward to seeing him at the hospital and wanted to look beautiful for him. They'd spoken and sent text messages for the past few days. He'd traveled out of town to oversee the production of the video games for the Winter Wonderland project and had arrived back that morning. He'd sent a sweet good-morning text message along with a picture of him and Hope that flew her to cloud nine ever since.

Finally satisfied with her hair, Blythe closed the closet and almost jumped as she saw Tiffani leaning against the open office door.

"Hey, girl," Blythe said. "I didn't know you were standing there." Walking over to her desk, she tossed her makeup bag on it and grabbed her belongings. Swiping her shades, she placed them over her eyes and slid her purse on her shoulder.

"Just got here. Ms. Bernice said you were preparing to leave for the day to work on the Winter Wonderland project." Tiffani tilted her head, and her face lit up with excitement. "Do you have a lunch date first that you forgot to tell me about? You look hot!"

"Nooo…why would you think that?" *Oh, my goodness. Am I about to lie to my best friend?*

"Because you wear makeup only when you're going out somewhere. You rarely wear it here."

Walking around the desk, she met Tiffani at the door and headed out to the hallway as she racked her brain for the best way to answer the question without lying. Closing her office door, she locked it and trekked down the hall with her friend. "No date. Just, um… Preston invited some of the Winter Wonderland committee to the children's hospital. There's a read-a-thon today." *Okay, so it's not quite a lie. He did say at the first meeting that he'd love for the committee members to visit with the children.*

"That's cool. He loves going. I've been a few times, but it's an overwhelming experience because it reminds me of when he was there and we almost lost him." Tiffani's expression turned solemn but quickly perked back up. "You really seem to love working on this project. I've never seen you so involved with something before besides your business. You're almost glowing."

Blythe laughed nervously. She wanted nothing more than to tell Tiffani about Prez, but she wasn't sure how to word it. She liked Preston a lot. She'd had a harmless crush on him for the past year but not enough to do anything about because she knew it wouldn't lead to anything. Now the tide had turned, and the desire he'd awakened in her beckoned her to explore her feelings for him. Usually she told Tiffani everything, but right now she couldn't.

Even though Tiffani would hint that Blythe would be the perfect woman for Preston to settle down with, she didn't want to risk ruining their friendship. If it didn't work out, would Tiffani blame her? Would she be upset? Would their relationship be strained if Prez turned out to be a dog and Blythe hated his guts? She wouldn't expect Tiffani to take sides; however, she wouldn't expect her to be comforting toward her, either. Tiffani loved her big brother. No, for now, she'd keep it to herself. Besides, she and Preston were taking it slow just in case they realized there was nothing between them. Then at least they could go back to normal without anyone knowing. Even though the thought saddened her a bit.

Shaking off the sadness that wanted to sink in, she put on a pleasant smile.

"Just excited about this time of the year. You know how much I love Christmas." Her cell phone vibrated in her hand, and she glanced down to see Preston's name and a picture with Hope on the screen. A wide beam reached across her face when she saw his name and his charming smile. Slipping the cell phone in her purse, she looked up to see Tiffani eyeing her.

"Girl, that was some smile. You sure you don't have a hot date later on? You're doing that glowing thing again," Tiffani said in a singsong tone. "I haven't seen you this cheery since you finally started making a sizable profit at the paint studio and you paid your Lexus off."

"Oh, girl. No… I mean…nothing I want to discuss right now. It's too early. Plus, you know I can't keep a man once they learn I'm not giving up the goods anytime soon," she joked. *Of course, your brother doesn't seem to mind.* "I'm taking it one day at a time." *There, I didn't lie. I'm just omitting part of the truth.*

"Mmm-hmm. Well, don't forget to RSVP for my Christmas party. Are you bringing a date? Perhaps the man who made your face light up like the Christmas tree at Macy's?"

"Uh…um…" She stopped as she felt the corners of her mouth rise a little too hard in a smile that was sure to give her away. "No… I doubt it. Just put me down for one."

"Mmm…okay. That's cool, but if you change your mind, just bring him. If not, Broderick has some single colleagues coming. You know the saying— don't bring sand to the beach. Who knows? Maybe you'll meet someone under the mistletoe. I'll make sure there's plenty hanging."

Blythe chuckled. "Yeah, maybe."

"What's funny is that this morning I called Preston to ask which of the females he's currently juggling he would escort to the party. He said that he wasn't juggling anyone at the moment and he was seeing one special lady who could turn into more. I couldn't believe it. First him and now you, and neither of y'all wants to discuss it. Too bad it's not you two together. I've always thought you'd be perfect for each other. We're best friends, but wouldn't it be cool to be sisters?"

"Girl, you're a mess." Blythe laughed a little too hard and halted abruptly. "So, it's not common for him to date just one girl at a time?" She tried to keep her question steady and in her usual casual tone when speaking of him. But her heart pumped hard against her chest, and she hoped Tiffani wasn't able to hear it. Blythe could hear the echo in her own ears. Was he referring to her or someone else? He did say he wasn't seeing anyone but her, but that didn't mean there weren't other women waiting in the wings. Single men like him usually had backup.

"Yeah, but he always has backup. I got the impression this wasn't the case. Weird, I suppose, but I know my brother. He sounded—" Tiffani stopped as a pretty smile graced her angelic face "—different, but in a good way. Plus, he said 'special lady,' but he wasn't going to divulge anything further, which surprised me because he tells me *everything*. Even things I don't want to know. Anyway, I'm excited to meet this mystery woman. He said I would adore her, and he's never said that."

"Oh…so he's bringing her to the party?"

"He said he would ask her and get back with me. Well, speak of the devil." Tiffani nodded toward the window.

Blythe glanced in the direction Tiffani was looking to see Preston's Range Rover pull up to the curb between the bakery and art studio. Hope had her head out the window in the backseat, enjoying the cool breeze, and she barked affectionately when the two ladies walked out the door.

"Hey, Prez," Tiffani greeted him as he jumped out of the SUV. "We were just talking about you."

He raised a curious eyebrow and looked between the two ladies. Blythe, who was rubbing Hope, shook her head to let him know she hadn't told Tiff about them.

"Really? What were you two chatting about?" he asked with a slight smirk as he glanced over Tiffani's head at Blythe with a knowing gaze that roamed over her winter-white Indian tunic.

Blythe tore her eyes immediately from him. He looked scrumptious in a pair of khaki dress slacks, a baby-blue sweater and a gray newsboy cap. A light after-five shadow graced his face, making him more manly and sexy, especially when she noticed a few grays sprinkled in. Sucking in her breath, she had to remind herself to stay calm even though she wanted to land a kiss on his yummy lips and throw the cap off to run her fingers through his hair.

"My upcoming Christmas party," Tiffani answered, giving her brother a hug. "And the fact that you may have a special—"

"And the Winter Wonderland project," Blythe interjected before Tiffani went any further. "I was telling Tiff how much I've enjoyed working on it. It's a humble feeling to be a part of something so wonderful for the children," she rambled in one breath.

"And I'm *really* glad you decided to," Preston said, resting his eyes once more Blythe. "I couldn't have done it without you or the rest of the committee."

Tiffani smiled and patted Blythe on the back. "I told you my best friend is a gem. A true gem."

"That she is. An angel sent from heaven. I described the vision in my head and she sketched it out perfectly. I can't wait for you to see the transformation, Tiff. It's beautiful. Absolutely beautiful. And I know my nephew is going to have a blast."

Blythe caught his intense stare, and she turned her attention back to Hope. Preston's dazzling smile and genuine compliment were making her antsy… and hot. She was grateful that the siblings continued talking. She was scared that if she opened her mouth again, incomprehensible words would spill out.

"Well, I can't wait, either. KJ and I will have to stop by soon. Trust me, he has been begging me to take him. Oh, and your goodies for the hospital are ready and packed up on the back counter, with some extra éclairs for you."

"Great. Blythe, do you want to ride with me? I can bring you back here. No point in taking two cars. I called you a few moments ago to ask but it went to your voice mail."

Dang it. Now Tiff is going to put one and one together. "Oh…no. I'm not coming back here, but thank you. I'll follow you to the hospital."

"Okay. I'll go grab the treats and we can jet."

He skedaddled inside, and Blythe hoped that Tiffani would follow suit, but she didn't. Instead, she leaned against the SUV and rested inquisitive eyes on Blythe, who chanted over and over in her head that she wasn't going to break. Thank goodness she had on her wide aviator shades even though it was partly cloudy.

"Sooo… I see you and Prez are finally getting along," Tiffani stated, wearing a huge grin.

"We've always gotten along." Blythe shrugged nonchalantly and prayed Tiffani wasn't deciphering the phone call situation, but Blythe knew her friend well, and that's exactly what she was doing. Plus, Tiffani's cousin, Sydney, was a criminal profiler and had given them tips on body language. She tried to remain calm and hold her body still.

"Mmm…if you call him flirting and you laughing and ignoring him getting along, then okay, but something is different."

"Tiffani, you're crazy."

"Nope, just hopeful. But like they say, miracles happen around Christmas," Tiffani sang in a joyful tone. "I guess I'll just sit back in my front row seat and observe."

"*Chica*, you're a mess, and that's why I love you. Watch Hope. I'm going to start my car. It's been sitting out in the cold all day. You know I like it nice and toasty when driving."

Tiffani twisted her mouth to the side. "Uh-huh… okay. Have fun…reading to the children."

"I will, girl." Blythe pivoted on the heel of her boot and headed briskly to her car. Once settled, she exhaled a long breath and was grateful for the dark tint on her windows. She started the engine and peered over to see Preston emerge with a huge box. Tiffani opened the trunk for him, and Blythe could tell by her friend's cheerful facial expression—and the glance toward her—that Tiffani was questioning her brother, as well. He threw his head back in laughter, kissed his sister's cheek and hopped into his SUV.

Moments later, he pulled up beside her car, and she rolled down her driver's window.

"Hey, baby girl. I think my sister is on to us."

"Mmm...she's pretty observant."

"Yep. It runs in the family. She mentioned a phone call you didn't answer before I arrived that made your face light up like Christmas lights. She swears it was me." He tapped his chin, and a cocky grin emerged. "Oh, wait, that was me calling you," he said with an arrogant wink.

"Maybe it was someone else," she said, slyly returning the wink. "You're not the only man I know. It could've been my male friend with the black truck."

A sexy smile raised up the left corner of his mouth. "I'm the only man who makes you beam the way you did when you saw my name flash across your cell phone screen."

"If you say so. Perhaps I'm juggling men," she teased. "You aren't the only man in Atlanta."

"Alright now, woman. I'm not the possessive type, but when I want something, I go after it, and once it's mine, that's it. I don't share."

"Mmm-hmm...but I'm not yours."

"Not yet."

As much as she liked the sound of that, she wasn't going to admit it.

"You're funny, Prez. Don't we have somewhere to be?"

"Yes, and we need to get a move on. I just wanted to see your pretty face first. We're going to take 285 to Peachtree Industrial and go all the way until we get to Peachtree Road."

"I'll follow you."

An hour later, they were settled in the children's hospital's play center, an area designated for the patients to have a break from their rooms if they weren't restricted to their beds, depending upon the treatments they were being administered. The room reminded Blythe of a kindergarten classroom with different centers, artwork on the walls and educational games and books to keep the children occupied. There were about a dozen elementary-age children settled on the floor or on oversized bean-bag chairs, each accompanied by a nurse, parent or volunteer. A volunteer was reading *How the Grinch Stole Christmas* as the children listened intently. Her heart became heavy as she watched the kids smiling and laughing along with the story. She couldn't imagine what they were going through, being so young and cycling through rounds of chemo and radiation treatments. Glancing at Preston, who was seated next to her in the back of the room, she slid her hand over to his and grasped it tight. He squeezed hers back and leaned over to her ear.

"Are you okay?" he whispered.

She nodded yes and smiled reassuringly. "I'm fine."

For the next two hours, they read, played games and did art activities until the director of the center announced it was almost time for dinner and the children were due back in their rooms soon. Upon saying her goodbyes, Blythe was glad she'd tagged along and looked forward even more to the Winter Wonderland project. Now she understood why he was doing the project.

"Thank you for inviting me," she said as they stood between their two vehicles in the visitors' parking lot. "It was enlightening and a little sad all at the same time. Now I see why you're so passionate about coming here."

"I was one of them at one time in my life. It's something that doesn't leave you. It just makes you stronger, and you see life more clearly."

"That's why you live your life to the fullest. I get it now. I do."

"I'm glad you do. I keep telling you I'm not a bad guy."

"I never said you were a bad guy, but I know your type, or at least, that's what I thought. I'm seeing a different side, though. I'm witnessing the side Tiffani is always telling me about. The kindhearted, gracious, unselfish one. The one that just comforted and prayed with a little girl's father because his daughter had a negative reaction to her medicine this morning. That's the one I didn't know existed."

He ran his finger down her cheek. "That's because I want you to see that side. All the sides of me," he whispered. "So, you're going over to the warehouse?"

"Yep. I spoke to Sasha earlier. The makeshift wall in the merry-go-round area is up, so I'll tackle painting the scenery today, or at least sketch it out. I'll have to paint at another time."

"You need some assistance?" he asked as if he wanted her to say yes.

"Honestly, no, but you can keep me company."

He tilted his hat to her. "I look forward to it. I'm going to drop Hope off at home, and I'll be there in an hour or so."

Yanking Blythe by the waist, Preston dropped his lips to hers in an enticing, ardent kiss, causing a relieved, satisfied moan to escape from her throat. She'd desired nothing more than to kiss him when he'd hopped out of his SUV earlier.

He hovered his lips over hers and rested his warm hands on either side of her face. His stare was intense, and she couldn't remember any other man ever gazing at her with so much vigor and affection before. It shook her to the core. She was treading unfamiliar, deep waters and was drowning fast in an abyss of desire and passion for a man who had awakened a longing in her since the moment she'd met him.

"I've wanted to do that all day...actually for the past two days, since I last saw you. Can't stop thinking about you, woman. Why is that, huh? Why are you literally driving me insane? Sure, I'm not going to lie, I've thought about you since I met you, but not like this. Now I can't concentrate at work, and I stay awake at night thinking about touching and kissing you again. Heck, I just want to see you again and be graced by your beautiful smile."

"Me, too. I don't know what's happening, either, but I'm very glad it is. Maybe I shouldn't have pushed you away all those times."

"No, everything happens when it's supposed to happen, in its own time." He kissed her once more, this time touching her lips briefly before capturing them for a long, sensual kiss.

Blythe was in a daze when he released her, and for a second, she forgot where she was and where she was supposed to be going.

He opened her car door and stepped back. "I'll see you in a few."

"Alright. Don't take too long." She slid into the car, and he closed the door. Chuckling, she remembered her destination and pushed the starter button for the engine. The kiss and his words had left her in a haze. She couldn't see straight, and her heart pounded swiftly. Either she was having symptoms of an upcoming health scare or she was falling for Preston. She kind of hoped it was the latter.

Preston entered the venue and was enthralled by the vision of loveliness in front of him. She stood with her back to him as she sketched out a snowman while rocking to Christmas songs that played through her cell phone sitting nearby on the floor.

Now he knew why he hadn't stopped thinking about her since the first moment he touched her lips. She was everything he'd ever wanted in a woman. Compassionate. Gracious. Intelligent. Challenging. Beautiful inside and out. He'd known she had those qualities beforehand, but Preston was at peace with not pursuing her seriously when he'd first met her. Like he'd told her earlier, everything happened when it was supposed to, and now their time had come. He was going to make her his.

Strolling over to her, he encircled his arms around her waist and landed a gentle kiss on her shoulder that released an intoxicating moan from her lips. "Hey, you."

Turning around to face him, she smiled and laid a smooch on his cheek before slipping back to her mural. "You just missed Devin. He stayed later to wait for the photo booths to be set up."

"They already arrived?" he asked as his eyes perused the warehouse.

"Yep. They're over in the arcade area. That's going to be so much fun for the kiddies. I remember my sisters and me taking pictures in one at a carnival. I did a charcoal sketch of it for my parents' anniversary one year. That's when my mom realized art wasn't just a hobby for me."

"No, you are very talented and creative. You truly made my vision come alive."

"Thank you."

"Do you want to test out one of the booths?"

"Sure. Let's do it."

She took off her protective hair scarf and shook her hair. It fell wild and unruly around her shoulders, and he loved it like that.

They rushed over to one of the photo booths and slid inside the cramped space. Setting her on his lap, he wrapped his arms around her waist as she circled hers around his neck.

"Comfortable, baby girl?"

"Yep."

"Alright, I'll push the button. Ready?"

"No, wait. Is there paint on my face? Is my hair okay? I know it's probably a wild bird's nest."

"Nope. It's lovely, and there isn't any paint on your face."

Okay. "I'm ready."

He pushed the Start button, and a few moments later, the camera flashed as they changed poses that ranged from fun to downright silly—forehead kisses, bunny fingers behind her head and goofy faces. They took three sheets of pictures before stopping. She was still laughing from him tickling her side, and he held her close until she calmed down. Swiping her hair from her face, he kissed her lips softly, which changed her cute giggles to sultry moans that caused him to probe his tongue deeper. He ravished her mouth as he familiarized himself with every part of it, and his hands moved along her body in the same fashion. Her succulent lips and an alluring tongue that wound around his in such an arousing manner caused a strain against his pants.

The woman in his embrace was sexy and sensual. Desirable. Seductive. He didn't know how the hell he was going continue to be around her without needing to explore every single inch of her, but there was so much more to her than just sex. So much more to their relationship besides sex. But he did want her. There was no denying that; however, he wanted her in a way that made her all his. With the other women he'd been intimate with, sex had always been at the forefront of the relationship. He didn't want to place Blythe in that category. When and if they ventured to that side, Preston wanted Blythe to be as ready and comfortable with the decision as he was.

His lips left hers and trailed along her neck and collarbone. Her erotic moans filled his ears with the sweetest music he'd ever heard. He loved the fact that she was enjoying herself. He wanted her to be carefree with him.

Through the thin material of her tunic, he felt her pebbled nipples hard against his chest, causing him to remind himself to take a cold shower or five when he arrived home. Preston's hand itched to finish untying the cord on the blouse that had come loose during their photo session. He held on to it instead, tight in his hand, as he palmed her hip with the other. When he felt her hand glide across his, he glanced down to see her pulling the cord with a haughty stare. The blouse parted and the tops of her breasts were peeking through her black bra. *Is she a mind reader?* He hoped not, considering the naughty ideas he was thinking up, which would constitute more than five cold showers.

"What? Are you scared to touch me?" she asked. "It's okay, Prez." She grabbed his hand, placed it on her breast and massaged it in a circular motion. "I'll let you continue on your own."

She settled her hands on his neck and stared at him with heated eyes. He continued his tongue journey down her collarbone and between her breasts. They were perfect, smooth butterscotch mounds. Firm and plump. Just right for his hands and tongue as he kissed along the outskirts of one of them before moving the cup of the bra down to expose the other one. Her head arched back as he licked and teased her nipple, which hardened even more. Then he took the majority of it into his mouth. She flung his hat off, wove her fingers into his hair and shifted his head to her other breast. He loved how she was a woman who knew exactly what she wanted and how she wanted it, which turned him on even more. He'd thought perhaps she'd be shy and resistant, but Blythe was fully aware of her sexuality.

His tongue and lips continued to drive her senseless as her moans and groans of pleasure erupted over and over. She squirmed in his lap and he tried to keep her still in the small, confined area, but the more he kneaded and teased her breasts, the more trembles tore through her body. Standing her up, he backed her against the small wall of the booth, which was just big enough for her to lean on. However, being six-foot-two, he couldn't stand with her, so he slid his tongue down her body until he reached the belt of her pants. Goodness, he wanted her, but this wasn't the time or place. He'd promised her and himself there was no rush.

"Please," she begged breathlessly as she fumbled with her belt. "Please."

"No, not yet, beautiful. Not tonight. You're not ready, but I would like to do something else." He ran his tongue over his lips. "I'd love to taste you. Can I, or is that against…?"

"No…do what you want, Prez. I don't care right now."

Chuckling, he finished unfastening her belt and slacks to expose black satin panties that matched her bra. "But I care about you very much. Do you hear me?"

"Yes."

He eased the wide-leg pants and panties down over her butt and hips until they fell to her ankle boots. She shifted in the confined space and reached down to toss the boots off, followed by the pants, all of which fell outside the booth.

Running a hand up her smooth leg, he ended at her center, causing her breathing to become erratic as he massaged her slowly but deeply. She moaned in a pleased, almost relieved way. He slipped a finger inside her, which stifled his breath as the warmth of her surrounded his skin. His thoughts zoomed him to a time in the future when he could ideally feel her tighten and clinched around something else. He figured tonight would be another cold shower night.

"That feels…mmm so damn wonderful, Prez… mmm…damn, baby," she mumbled as her body shuddered and she clutched his shoulders. She stared down at him with an ardent gaze.

He chuckled. "Well, I can only imagine what you're going to be like when I glide my tongue on you."

"Stop teasing me and just do it," she demanded. "What are you waiting for?"

"Be patient, baby girl."

"Do you know how long it's been?"

"Exactly, which is why I'm going to take my time savoring you. I want to satisfy you completely. It's all about you right now, beautiful."

Blythe tried to stand up straight against the small wall space, but it was no use, as she found herself sliding down and then back up. Her knees buckled every single time Preston's finger would glide out and then back inside, causing her right leg to tremor. She couldn't believe she'd actually pleaded with him for more, but she was grateful that he possessed more willpower than she did. She couldn't help it. For the first time in a long while, a man finally made her feel alive and sensual. She'd always enjoyed sex and intimacy, but after being in relationships that weren't going anywhere, Blythe could no longer fathom having meaningless sex. It was supposed to be special, and she yearned for a heart-and-soul connection with a man. She yearned to make love with a man. Anything outside that would be that one word she never said in front of her parents.

Blythe faded so far into oblivion that when Preston replaced his finger with his tongue, the start of an orgasm shot through her veins. Her moans escalated higher and he increased his speed, circling around her and running his tongue between her other lips until he reached the opening and licked his way inside. She held on to his shoulders as he grasped her buttocks and slid her body over to sit on the bench. Lifting her legs over his shoulders, he never missed a beat as he continued to wreak pure wonderful mayhem on her. She glanced down at him and noted how intent and focused he was on pleasing her. Preston's groans relayed to her that he was enjoying himself, as well.

He raised his burning eyes to hers momentarily and winked with a wicked smile. "You good, baby? Are you enjoying yourself?"

"Yes…and you?" Her question came out in a hoarse manner, thanks to all the sounds she had no control over.

"Oh, yeah…" He paused, licking between her folds and holding her hips still as she nearly rose off the seat. "Oh, yeah. You are absolutely delicious. I can't get enough."

Preston delved in again, but this time the orgasm that was near stormed through her, and she rose off the seat. He managed to keep his tongue on her, which drove Blythe even more insane, and another orgasm crashed through her and tormented her to no end. This time he grabbed her to him as she shuddered in his protective embrace. He placed kisses on her forehead and gently rubbed her center until her breathing calmed down. It wasn't back to normal, but she was finally able to open her eyes to find him gazing at her with an affectionate expression. She smiled weakly and nestled her head on his chest. His heart was beating almost as rapidly as hers, not that she was shocked. He'd put in a lot of work as well, and if they ever went further and it was any more intense than their episode a moment ago, she wasn't sure she could handle him.

But she did want to experience more with him. Not tonight. He was right. She wasn't ready, but she was appreciative that Preston was the kind of man who respected her and would not ask her to go any further just to satisfy his needs.

"Hey there," he whispered. "Are you awake? You're quiet."

"I'm fine." She raised her head to look at him. "Just thinking."

"About?"

"Us. I almost can't believe this is happening. That we're kind of happening, you know?"

"Yeah, we are, huh? I've enjoyed every moment

we've spent together, and I'm looking forward to many more."

"Me, too, but for right now, I need to finish sketching out the mural. Mandi and Allison are coming in the morning to paint it with me before we head to work."

"I guess we got carried away, huh?"

She lifted off him and stood as best as she could. Her legs were wobbly, and she was so relaxed from their tryst, she really wanted nothing more than to cuddle in his arms and fall asleep.

"We did and I enjoyed it, but now we have work to do, or at least, *I* have work to do, but it shouldn't take long. It's just snowmen."

Moments later, she was back to sketching, and Preston decided to conduct a walk-through to see what still needed to be done. She caught herself staring at him and not believing all of this was happening. Once the skiing snowmen were complete, she settled on the floor in front of the panel. Soon he sat next to her and placed a tender kiss on the side of her neck, jolting a few tingles that lingered from earlier.

"Ready?" he asked, scanning he mural.

"Yep." She stretched her arms out and yawned. "I'm going to sleep well tonight."

"Thanks to me," he bragged, brushing invisible dust off his shoulder.

"You're a mess. You'll probably be taking a cold shower."

"Touché, beautiful. You know, I was thinking

about going skydiving sometime soon, probably before the event. I haven't done it in a few months. It's a good way to release pent-up energy, and it's a wonderful high. You wanna come?"

Her heartbeat ceased for a second at the thought of jumping out of an airplane. "Uh…you mean to watch you from my safe spot on the ground, right? Take pictures? Sure, I'll videotape it for you," she suggested, because she sure as hell wasn't going to jump.

"No… I mean jump with me," he said matter-of-factly. "It'll be cool."

Cool? More like insane. Sarcastic laughter rose loud from her throat, which was slightly scratchy from her wild moans earlier. "Wait… Prez… I've never skydived before or had any aspirations to do so. It's not on my bucket list. How about I just tag along for moral support?"

"I guess…but think about it. It could fun."

"Yeah…free-falling to my death isn't my idea of fun. How about you create a skydiving video game? I promise to be the first to test it."

"Babe, even Hope and my dog before her have gone with me. I've done it too many times to count. I'm not a ghost sitting in front of you."

"No…but…oh, my goodness…" She ran her fingers through her hair and shook off the jitters that prickled along her skin. "I'm nervous just thinking about it."

"Scared of heights?" he asked.

"No, scared my parachute won't open and I'll

land splat against the ground. And then my parents would kill me again for dying, and you, too. Definitely you."

"Relax. We can do it together. Literally. We will be strapped together. It's called tandem jumping. It's for first-timers. I'm certified, so you'll be fine. I promise."

"First-timers? Like I'd ever do it again…*if* I agreed to this. That wasn't a yes."

"I think you'd enjoy it—otherwise I wouldn't have asked. I have videos of me you can watch, and I'll tell you everything you need to know beforehand. I promise."

"You've done this with other women?"

"No. You would be the first. I've jumped with my dad, Braxton and Sydney. Can't get my mother or Tiffani to go at all. Not even to watch. KJ wants to do it as soon as he's eighteen, even though Tiff isn't in agreement. I usually jump on my birthday and my skydiving buddies' birthdays, but for some reason, I want to do it now…with you. Will you think about it?"

Sighing, she pressed down more nervous tingles. "I'll go with you, but I can't promise you that I'm going to jump."

"Fair enough. I'll make the arrangements, and in the meantime, I'll email you some training videos to watch."

"Okay, and you won't be mad if I say no?"

Grasping her hand, he squeezed it tight. "No, precious, I won't be mad. I really don't know why the idea popped into my head, but I'd love for you to share that experience with me. It's exhilarating. It's a natural high I can't explain. Sort of like those climaxes you just had, but better."

"Ha… I don't think I could handle anything better than that."

A naughty grin emerged from him as he stood and then held out his hands to pull her up. He drew her toward him, and she sank naturally into his arms as if she was meant to be there.

"My dear, that was just a sample. If we ever have…make love, you'll learn that was the tip of the iceberg. There are so many other things to explore."

"I'll be sure to be well-rested when the occasion arises, and I'll think about the skydiving adventure."

"That's all I ask."

Chapter 7

Blythe stared out the window of the small plane that flew over north Georgia. It was two weeks after Preston had asked her to skydive with him, and she still hadn't quite agreed to, even though she was dressed in a skydiving jumpsuit, helmet, goggles and gloves along with the harness that would eventually be connected to Preston. She held his hand for dear life as he chatted casually with his friend and instructor, Charles, who was going to jump with them and tape it. She'd watch the training video at least twenty-five times in the past week. She now knew the correct free-fall position, how to exit the plane, when and how to open the parachute and how to land...that was the part she was looking forward to the most.

Even though the thought of being strapped to Preston was kind of cool, too.

The past few weeks had been full of painting, working and spending her free time with Preston. She'd enjoyed every moment with him and was antsy and annoyed when she was away from him. The Winter Wonderland festivities were over a week away, and everything was on schedule. She looked forward to the events…that is, if she survived today. She exhaled and squeezed his hand tighter while saying a prayer. She'd informed her oldest sister what she was doing today so someone in her family would know if it didn't end well.

Preston leaned over to her and kissed her cheek. "You good, baby girl?"

Scooting closer to him, she linked her arm with his. "You mean scared? Yes…make that hell, yes."

"I promise, I got you," he reassured her with a trustworthy smile. "I wouldn't have brought you if I didn't think you could handle it."

"We're almost at our jumping point and need to get ready," Charles said and proceeded to stand by the door.

"Well?" Preston asked, standing and holding out his hand to her.

She unbuckled her seat belt and grabbed his hand. "Okay."

He scooped her up in his arms. "I promise you won't regret it, and who knows? Perhaps the next time, we can jump holding hands, staring at each other."

"One jump at a time, bruh. It's way too soon to discuss another one."

"Gotcha, babe."

Seconds later, they were harnessed together as she stood in front of Preston at the door that the flying assistant, Ray, was about to open. Blythe couldn't believe she was preparing to jump out of a plane at fourteen thousand feet in the air. But since Preston was behind her, she felt secure, and it wasn't because they were heavily strapped together. She couldn't explain the overwhelming emotions that soared through her. It hit her hard when Ray opened the plane's doors and the rush of air flew in. There was no turning back now.

"Ready to jump, baby girl?" Preston shouted loud in her ear, moving them up as they stood in the correct jumping position.

"Yes," she screamed back.

"You trust me, right?"

She glanced at him over her shoulder. "With all my heart." And she meant every word.

Smiling, he kissed her tenderly as her eyes fluttered shut, and for a moment, she was lost in a free-falling abyss, surrounded by his protective embrace. Sighing, she turned back around, and when she opened her eyes they were indeed falling…out of the plane. She screamed at the top of her lungs with enjoyment as they soared together in laughter. Even though she couldn't hear anything, she knew he had to be laughing with her.

Blythe couldn't believe it was really happening, but Preston was right. It was truly a natural high. As a child, she'd dreamed she could fly with the birds, and now it was happening with him. Soaring above the earth was indeed invigorating and thought-provoking. The sky had never appeared so blue before. White pillows of clouds swooshed past them, which was the coolest thing ever. The phrase *on cloud nine* took on new meaning because that's what she was experiencing at that very moment. She tried to photograph all the images in her head so they could lend ideas for a picture she would paint of her magical experience.

Charles was with them as well with the video camera, and she gave two thumbs-up and a loud woo-hoo that she couldn't hear as they continued to free-fall at one hundred twenty miles per hour. She could see for miles and miles, and the view was incredible. It was different than flying on an airplane. She was actually a part of the sky and the atmosphere. She felt one with nature and with Preston.

About five thousand feet before they were to land, Preston opened the parachute, and they drifted to the ground, much to her dismay. The adrenaline rush was revitalizing. It had ended way too soon. She wanted more. Now she understood why Preston sky-dived, and she couldn't wait to do it again with him.

Landing standing up, they tumbled over in laughter. Preston kissed the back of her neck, and she closed her eyes as the sensation of falling hadn't left her yet.

"Can we can go again?" she asked in between her giddy laughs.

"I take it you enjoyed yourself?"

"Mmm-hmm… I did."

"I knew that you would."

He helped her stand up as one of the workers rushed over to help them out of their harnesses. Afterward she fell into Preston's arms and exhaled.

"That was awesome, absolutely awesome. I swear I could go again right now. I see why you love it. It's like… I can't explain it. It's just a powerful, organic experience that I'm glad I was able to share—" she paused as she felt herself smile "—with you. You made it the most unforgettable experience ever. I can't think of a time when I've felt so carefree and one with the universe. I didn't want it to end."

"Now you see why I do it. Sooo…you really want to go again? Right now?" he questioned with a puzzled expression.

"For sure. Right now."

"Let's do it."

After a refreshing shower, Blythe crashed on the couch next to Preston in her living room as her high and heart rate finally settled down. They'd skydived again, and that time she'd opened the chute and steered it down to the ground.

"I still can't believe we did it again," he said, reaching over for her hand and squeezing it. "I'm so glad you enjoyed yourself."

"I truly did. That was one of the best experiences ever, and I have you to thank. I called my sister Brandi after I got out of the shower. She couldn't believe I went through with it. Twice."

"Well, I can. You were amazing. So, your whole family lives in Brooklyn?"

"No, not now. Just my parents and baby sister. Brandi lives in Chicago with her husband."

"Had you planned on going home for the holidays?"

"Not this year. My parents and baby sis are going on a cruise, and Brandi and her husband are spending it with her in-laws. She's not looking forward to it, but they agreed on every other Christmas with their families."

"Well, the Chase family is having dinner at Megan's this year. You're welcome to join us."

"Actually, I am. Tiffani invited me a while ago."

"I see. How about we have a light brunch at my place that morning? Exchange gifts and chill until it's time to head to Megan's?"

"That sounds like a plan." She was almost finished with his present. It just needed a few final touches. "And I'll cook."

"No. It's Christmas. Just bring yourself. I'll handle the rest."

"No argument from me. I'll bring a red velvet

cake, though. It's the only dessert I know how to make well. It's my dad's favorite, and I usually make it for him on Christmas Day."

"I love red velvet cake. It's one of my favorite desserts." Preston raised a wicked eyebrow and licked his lips. "But you want to know what my new favorite dessert is?" He ran a finger across her lips, and she sucked it into her mouth.

"Mmm...me? It had better be me," she joked, pinching his cheek.

"Oh, it is. All of you."

Climbing onto his lap, Blythe straddled him and placed her hands around his neck. She brushed her lips against his, and a sensual moan released from her when his hands roamed down to her butt and pressed her hard against him. She could feel the hardness of his manhood through her flimsy nightgown, and she kicked herself for not putting on the thick flannel one. Butterflies rustled in her stomach, and waves of passion raced through her body as their kiss intensified. She was free-falling again, but this time the high was even more invigorating than skydiving two times in a row. Her lips left his and slid down his neck. Licking and nibbling his warm skin turned her on even more, especially when his erotic groans filled the air. Today's events had heightened the soulful connection they shared. She wanted him now more than anything, and she wasn't disappointed with herself, either. It was her decision. Always had been.

"Damn, woman," he groaned, weaving his fingers in her hair. "I didn't know you were this aggressive…and I love it." Preston arched his neck back even more as she continued placing seductive kisses on him.

She snickered. "So I hear, loud and clear."

"But… I… You've got stop tempting me, woman."

She faced him and rested her hands on his chest. Lowering her lips to his, she whispered, "Maybe I don't want to stop. Maybe I need you. No turning back."

His forehead indented, and he shifted under her. "Blythe…"

"I'm ready if you are, and I know you are. It's written all over your face, Prez, and you're hard as a rock." Grinding on him, her breath caught in her throat. He was bigger than she'd realized, and he grew the more she swirled around on him.

He grasped her hands and kissed them, and a sincere yet serious expression reached his face. "Babe, I've been ready since our first kiss, but I don't want you to do anything you'd regret."

She shook her head. "I'm not going to regret it. I want to be with you in every way possible."

"And I want the same, but you know this will change the dynamics of our relationship, baby girl."

"I'm aware of that. They've already changed, which is why we're having this conversation…and wasting precious time."

"So, I guess you've sensed that I've fallen for you?"

"I have, and I've fallen for you, as well."

"Do you know how long I've searched for a woman like you? You're a godsend."

Sliding off his lap, she reached her hand out to him. "Well, the search is over. I'm all yours."

Instead of grabbing her hand, he stood and lifted her up in one swoop. Carrying her to the bedroom, he laid her down on the comforter and slid his body over hers. They stared at each other for a few moments before she reached her lips up to his and kissed him. Fluttering her eyes shut, she was once more transported into an abyss of floating among the clouds. His loving embrace had to be the safest place on earth.

When they were skydiving, she'd never felt so protected by a man before. She'd trusted him with all her heart. She'd experienced the emotions and adrenaline rush not because she'd jumped from an airplane but because she was with him on another level that she couldn't explain. She needed to feel all of him. Needed to be one with him because their connection had grown in every way. Heart. Body. Soul. She didn't have any doubts or any regrets. And like him, she could admit to herself she'd been ready for him since the first moment his lips touched hers. In that moment, he'd awakened a desire and passion in her that she'd buried in her mind and heart.

Preston sat up and began to unbutton his shirt. A

wide grin crossed her face at his glorious rippling muscles. She wrapped her legs around his waist, and his lips met hers again in a fierce, amorous kiss. She clutched his shoulders and let the feel of him on her immerse her into a surreal oblivion as their fervor increased with each passing second.

He slid his tongue down to her neck and then to her cleavage. He dragged her nightgown up by the hem in one swoop and lifted it over her head to expose her breasts, which craved his tongue on them. He sank his mouth onto one of the hardened nipples, and she sighed out his name in relief. She roamed her hands over his hard chest, which could easily substitute as a washboard if her washing machine ever stopped working. She didn't know how much longer she could hold on before demanding that they skip the foreplay, but he was a passionate and skilled lover, so she wanted to savor every moment of their first time together.

His lips continued making their way down her chest, stomach, belly button and ended up on the top of her panties. He rested his heated stare on her. She nodded the go-ahead, and he slid the panties off with his teeth. Standing, he took off his pants and boxers, and she gulped—this time at the length and hardness of him. She watched as he reached back for his pants, sifted through his wallet and pulled out two gold packets.

Winking, he rejoined her on the bed and placed the packets under a pillow.

"You just happen to have those on hand?" she teased.

"I started to carry them after our time in the photo booth."

"Good thinking."

He captured her lips once more in a slow, unhurried kiss that sent heat waves of passion soaring through her. A tremble erupted over her entire body as she realized she was about to be one with Preston. She was nervous and excited all at the same time. This would indeed change the dynamics of their relationship; however, she'd never felt this carefree with a man before.

Lifting his head, he stared down at her with a concerned expression. "I just want to make sure you're okay. It's not too late to change your mind."

She smiled, patting his cheek, and thought how lucky she was that she'd found a man who cared. "I'm fine, babe. Honestly. Trust me, I would tell you if I wasn't."

"Just checking. I don't want you to feel bad afterward or think that you made a mistake."

"I'm not a virgin or a prude."

She pulled his head down to hers and kissed him furiously to show him just how much she was ready for him. He let out a growl as she ground her hips on him. Reaching over to the pillow, he pulled out a condom packet.

"I'm taking the hint," he mumbled, kissing the side of her neck before lifting up.

Her body ached with sheer delight as she waited for him to finish. She wrapped her legs around his waist and inhaled as he gently circled his tip around her center while staring directly at her. A low moan escaped her throat as he slid partway inside and then again as he nestled himself completely inside her. He didn't move.

"You're beautiful," he whispered. "So beautiful, and I'm a lucky man to have you in my life."

"Thank you."

Imprisoning her lips once more, he began to move slowly inside her at the same pace of their kissing. She remained still at first as he guided himself in and out of her at a sensual speed that sent emotional shudders to amplify with each stroke. Once she was comfortable, she began to meet his thrusts, which caused him to shake against her.

"Damn..." he groaned. "You feel so good, baby girl."

"Mmm...you, too."

Her hips began to gyrate even more on him, and the intensity of being connected caused a powerful orgasm to rip through her. She held on to him tightly as once again she was above the clouds with him, flying above the earth in the most thrilling high of her life. When she finally landed, he kissed her forehead and smiled down at her with loving eyes. That's when she knew she wouldn't regret her decision. There was no doubt in her mind that he was the one.

"Hi there," he said. "You good, babe? That was some tremor."

"Yes...so good. Don't stop yet."

Chuckling, he began to thrust into her again, but this time their speed increased as he delved in and out with deep strokes that she happily welcomed over and over for a long while, until he shuddered uncontrollably against her and let out a roar along with a slew of curse words. He breathed hard into the side of her neck with a heavy pant as aftershocks still trembled through him. Her wobbly legs fell from around his waist and spread out onto the bed, but her hands never relaxed from clenching his shoulders as her climax still tingled in her center.

After their breathing calmed down a tad, Preston turned them over and adjusted her so that they could face each other. He cupped her face and kissed her gently on the lips as the last of her tingles finally ended. Snuggling her head against his chest, he held her close. His heartbeat raced, and she listened to it until it simmered back down to a normal rate.

Sometime later, after another sensual round of lovemaking, she found herself under the covers, still wrapped in his embrace. Glancing over him, she squinted her eyes in the dark to read the digital clock on the nightstand. 1:30 a.m.? *Geez, how long have we been asleep?*

"Hey, you," he greeted her in a sleepy tone.

"Hi," she whispered.

"Are you alright?" he asked.

"I'm perfect, just exhausted and thirsty."

"Well, we did a lot of sweating."

"I don't remember falling asleep."

"Yeah, you dozed off soon after. You've had a long day. You went skydiving. Twice."

"Mmm…four times. Making love with you is like being above the clouds again."

"Wow. That's the best compliment I've ever heard." Sitting up, he jumped out of the bed, turned on the lamp and slid on his pants.

Her heart dropped. *Was he leaving?*

"Going to get you some water. Do you want anything to eat?"

Did he hear the question in my head? Or maybe it was written on my face.

"Um…there are some grapes in the fridge." Her chest relaxed, and she was able to breathe again. "Grab whatever you want."

"Alright. I'll be back, my lady."

After he left, she took a quick shower and strolled back into the bedroom to find him sitting propped up against the pillows with a tray of grapes and cheese and a bottled water on her nightstand.

"Thank you," she said with a wince as she hopped back into the bed.

"Are you okay?"

"Just a little sore. It's been a while, but I'll be fine." She grabbed the water bottle and took a long swig. "It was worth every single minute." Pausing, she took another gulp and then turned to him. "Do you have to leave soon to check on Hope? You've been gone all day."

He stopped midbite of a piece of cheddar cheese. "Trying to kick a brother out?" He laughed. "Nah… I had my assistant feed her and take her outside." Reaching over her, he slid his cell phone off the nightstand. "And I have cameras in my home." He pressed an app on his phone and showed Blythe. "See, she's sleeping on the couch, where she shouldn't be, but that's okay. That's where I sit and watch television."

"She misses you."

"Yeah, but she's sound asleep. Plus, Linda arrives at JP3 Chase tomorrow morning at seven. I'll just send her a message to check on Hope. Linda knows what to do."

"I've been meaning to ask you, why the initials JP3?"

He frowned. "Oh…you didn't know? Those are my initials. I'm named after my father. John Preston Chase III. Growing up, everyone called me Prez or Preston. Sometimes Tre."

"So, John is your first name?"

"Yep, but no one ever calls me that except my parents when I was in trouble. When my mom would use my full government name, I knew it couldn't be good."

Popping a grape into her mouth, she snickered. "I'm sure that was often, huh?"

"Yeah… I mean, I was a good kid overall, but you know, I was on the nerdy side with a smart mouth. I thought everything that came out of it was correct. Teachers don't always find that amusing, and considering I was raised by two educators, going to school with them was no fun, especially when my dad was also my principal in high school."

"I'll bet it wasn't, but be glad your dad wasn't an accountant. My dad tracked every little penny I spent starting when I was five years old. My five-dollar allowance went a long way. However, now I appreciate it. I'm a stickler for staying on budget and not buying overly expensive things."

Blythe glanced at the cell phone again to look at Hope, who had jumped off of the couch and now lay by the elevator.

Sighing, she ran her finger on the screen. "Aw… she's waiting for you."

Frowning, he looked and then shook his head with a smirk. "You want me to leave, don't you?"

"No, babe," she answered, squeezing his hand. "I just get sentimental over dogs, especially at this time of year. My German shepherd died two Decembers ago, and I've had other dogs as well, growing up."

"Well, you did say you were contemplating owning another one soon."

"Yeah, I'm ready."

Tapping his chin, he nodded his head. "Yeah, you are. I'll tell you what. I'll go home, but only if you come with me. I need to hold you tonight."

"That sounds perfect."

Chapter 8

Blythe checked her curls and makeup one more time in the rearview mirror before unlocking the car and letting the valet parking attendant open the door. She quickly snatched the evening clutch that matched her fiery red after-five dress and wrap from the passenger seat. Sliding out of the car, she greeted the young man who handed her a ticket and walked up the stairs onto the vast porch of Broderick and Tiffani Hollingsworth's mansion, which was superbly decorated for Christmas. White-and-gold lights were intertwined in the evergreen shrubs that flanked both sides of the cobblestone driveway, evergreen garlands with red ribbon woven through wrapped around the humongous white columns, and the double doors were covered with two gigantic wreaths with holly, baby's breath and red poinsettias.

As she entered, a waiter greeted her with a tray of champagne, but she shook her head no and continued on, nodding and waving at people she did and didn't know. Her eyes perused the festive crowd as she searched for Preston. They'd left their respective homes at the same time, but she figured he'd beat her there because even though she lived closer, he had a tendency to drive his two-door Aston Martin like it was a race car.

They still hadn't told anyone they were seeing each other, and that was fine with her for the time being, even though he was ready to go public with it. After their lovemaking session that morning, her body still radiated aftershocks like an earthquake. She wasn't sure she had enough willpower to contain herself in his presence tonight if he showed up drop-dead gorgeous.

And she knew that would be likely, because the man looked excruciatingly hot in a tux. She'd attended Braxton's wedding a few months ago, and when Preston walked down the aisle, she had to do a double take. Later on at the reception, he'd approached her to say hello and, of course, flirt. Brushing him off with a laugh wasn't as easy as usual. She'd found herself gazing at him for the rest of the evening as he'd danced and flirted with Elle's single friends. She could honestly admit that was the first time she considered going out with him, but then blamed it on having one too many glasses of champagne. Plus, weddings always made her a tad sentimental and placed her in a romantic state.

"There you are," a bubbly female voice exclaimed. "You look radiant, girl."

Blythe turned to gaze at Tiffani, who looked dazzling in a pink sequined minidress. Her waist-length hair was up in a side ponytail with cascading curls that fell around her left shoulder. A diamond choker graced her neck, and a matching tennis bracelet encircled her wrist. Sometimes Blythe forgot her friend was married to a multimillionaire who lavished expensive gifts on her all the time. Tiffani was still the same humble, hardworking, independent woman she'd met three years ago. Being married to a millionaire hadn't changed her at all.

"And so do you, *chica*," Blythe complimented her, hugging her best friend and finally spotting Preston over her shoulder at the bar, chatting with Broderick and Braxton. Preston raised his champagne glass, and his knowing, seductive gaze sent goose bumps over her skin. He was indeed sexy and commanding in his Elle Lauren tuxedo. She wanted to rip it off him and extinguish the blaze that burned on her skin.

"Thank you, but your dress is smoking hot with the side slit, *and* it's backless...mmm-hmm. You're going to drive some single man in here crazy tonight. There's plenty of mistletoe around, so don't get caught under it. No, wait. I don't mean that. Let's go grab something to eat. I'm famished after running around making sure everything is perfect for my guests."

Tiffani pulled her by the hand and led Blythe to a massive spread with just about every appetizer and dish on the planet.

"Everything looks delish. I don't know where to start," Blythe said, grabbing a plate. She glanced up to find Preston staring at her as if she was the only person in the room. She sucked in her breath and suppressed the smile that wanted to emerge. She kept her attention focused on placing quiche and shrimp puffs on her plate while trying to keep her shaky hands steady.

"Thank you. Of course, I can't take any credit for it. Chef Crenshaw and his staff did all of this. Oh... I need to go check on KJ and his friends in the media room. Preston brought over his latest video game to keep them occupied. I'll be right back. Let's sit out on the veranda. The twins and Elle are out there."

After Tiffani left, Blythe finished piling food on her plate and turned to head for the bar for a drink, only to find Preston standing behind her, holding two glasses of champagne. His commanding demeanor and naughty smirk warmed her skin even more.

He leaned toward her ear. His tongue flicked across it and that subtle contact sent her mind back to their sensual session that morning in the shower. It was supposed to kill time since they both were running late for appointments. Instead, they made love, and Blythe was an hour late to her hair appointment with a relaxed grin on her face. Her hairdresser questioned it the entire time, but she remained mum.

Clearing his throat, Preston whispered, "You look radiant, baby girl. Can't wait to get you back to my place after the party ends, or before it ends. Not really in the mood to schmooze tonight. I'd rather be alone with you."

"Who says I'm coming over?" Winking, she took one of the glasses and swished away before forgetting about everybody else and laying a kiss on him. She headed to the veranda to join Elle and the twins, Megan and Sydney, Tiffani's cousins who were married to the Monroe brothers.

Megan waved and stood to hug Blythe while Sydney, who was seven months pregnant, nodded with food in her mouth. Elle gave her a warm hug, and two other ladies Blythe didn't know greeted her as she sat at the round table with a beautiful arrangement of different colored poinsettias in the center.

"So wonderful to see you, Blythe," Megan greeted, then sipped her champagne. "I hear you're working on Preston's project. Sasha and Devin have done nothing but praise you."

"It's been fun. I'm surprised you aren't assisting."

"I wanted to, but with the show taping right now, I've been out of the state since after Thanksgiving, decorating flipped houses, and we just taped a holiday special that airs tomorrow. But I'm home until after the New Year, and then back on the road to do ten more episodes of *Fix My Flipping Disaster*."

"Can't wait. It's one of my favorite shows. Some of those houses are in horrible shape. That last episode, I just knew you were going to burn it and start from scratch."

Megan giggled. "Yeah, I believe that was my first thought when I saw the rats staring me down like they wanted to cut me for invading their space. And then when Jonathan knocked down that wall only to expose all those wasp nests, I kept thinking maybe this wasn't a great idea."

"Well, the house is gorgeous now, thanks to you and the crew from Supreme Construction. And I know you're glad to be home with your family for the holidays."

"I am. Steven is off from the senate until the session begins in January, so it's just us and the twins. Luckily my baby girls can travel with me. Otherwise I'd go crazy missing them. Now I'm just ready to be an auntie to my nephew." Megan reached over and rubbed Syd's stomach. "And an auntie to my niece." She smiled at Braxton's wife, Elle, four months pregnant, seated across from her. "If Tiffani gets pregnant again soon, we'll have a family full of babies."

Sydney nodded as she finished chewing her food. "Yep, and if Preston ever settles down and gets married, add a few more. He always said he wanted three children."

Blythe nearly choked on the chocolate-covered strawberry in her mouth. Three children? Not that they had discussed marriage, or having kids, for that matter, but she'd always wanted three children, as well. She glanced up to spot Preston once more staring at her as if he wanted to rip her dress off. He was chatting and sipping bourbon with Braxton, Broderick and Bryce, Syd's husband, on the other side of the veranda. He bowed his head before returning his attention back to his conversation. Every now and then she'd catch him glance her way, and a naughty yet charming smile would form on his ruggedly handsome face.

Blythe tried to chime in to the conversation at her table about baby furniture, strollers and diapers, but she couldn't concentrate as she sensed his gaze on her. Like him, she was halfway ready to leave so they could be alone. She'd never cared for big, fancy parties anyway. She'd rather be at Preston's loft, cuddling and watching Christmas movies…after making love.

Her thoughts drifted back to their time in the shower, which kept her pretty much in her own world. She no longer heard the conversation. However, when one of the ladies she didn't know mentioned Preston's name in a sultry tone, her ears perked up again. She jerked her head immediately to the lady with the boobs spilling out of a dress that was a size too small. Blythe hoped that she could contain her composure and not give off any signs that there was something between her and Preston.

The lady sipped her champagne and cut her eyes seductively in Preston's direction. "Your fine cousin

Preston keeps staring over here. He knows he misses me and the things we did…well, it wasn't that long ago," she said, running her hand sensually across her chest. "It was just last month, but it's time for seconds…well, thirds, actually. It was a long, wild night with him."

Sydney chuckled sarcastically and leaned toward her. "Marissa, what makes you think Prez is looking at you?" she asked with a condescending expression.

Marissa flipped her hair with a huff. "Trust me, I know when a hungry man is staring me down like a piece of prime steak. I purposely wore this dress tonight just for him. Green is his favorite color on me. He says it brings the flecks of green out of my brown eyes."

Megan and Elle laughed, but Blythe remained quiet and simply nodded with a smile. The things Preston had told women could all be compiled in a book entitled *How to Make a Woman Think She's the Only One.*

Sydney didn't laugh and stated in a serious manner, "Mmm-hmm, well, I'm no expert…oh, wait, I *am* the top criminal profiler for the Georgia Bureau of Investigation." She paused, leaning even further over the table to Marissa. "Trust me, sweetheart, he's not looking at you." Syd glanced at Blythe before standing with her plate. "I'm going to grab some cheesecake for the baby."

Marissa smacked her lips after Sydney left. "Whatever. I know when a man wants me. Her hormones are just making her say mean things. Besides, I sent him a text message and some racy pictures of me in my birthday suit moments ago. We're meeting up after the party. So trust me, he is definitely staring at me. Why do you think he keeps looking over here with that sexy, mischievous grin? And who else is he looking at? He's related to all of you." Standing, she grabbed her clutch and her empty plate. "Going to go schmooze and mingle for a bit and then head home and wait for Mr. Chase. Toodles, ladies."

The delicious food in Blythe's mouth lost all of its taste as soon as Marissa mentioned Preston. Was he staring at the voluptuous, sexy woman? Blythe caught his eyes sway Marissa's way as she sashayed with an extra dip of her hips back into the great room. Well, she had her answer and tried to hold in the anger that wanted to erupt. Instead, she put on a pleasant smile as best she could when Tiffani approached, slammed into the chair next to her and started to ramble about the pastry chef she'd hired for the occasion messing up her recipe for eggnog cupcakes and stating she should've just made them herself.

But Blythe hardly heard her. She couldn't believe that she'd trusted Preston. She thought he could possibly be the one, but now this was just a reminder that a cheetah's spots would never change. Preston was a player. He loved the attention and his sexual encounters with different women. But she couldn't blame him. She could only blame herself for actually believing that he cared for her when all he really wanted was sex. Heck, he probably got a kick out of her sitting next to Marissa. Two of the women he was juggling sitting next to each other and not knowing it had to be a real turn-on for him. Probably the reason for his devilish grin.

Seething in silence, Blythe comforted Tiffani, who was upset about the cupcakes that weren't going to be used. It helped her to restrain herself from going over to Preston and cursing him out in front of everyone.

Sipping his bourbon, Preston frowned at the naked pictures on his cell phone as he erased them with Broderick and Braxton watching in utter disbelief. Yes, Marissa had an amazing body—he wasn't even going to deny that—but she and the pictures weren't doing anything to stir him. There was only one woman he wanted now, and she sat directly in his view.

"So, I'm assuming you aren't interested in her?" Broderick pried. "I didn't know you two were dating—or rather, had dated."

"We never did," Preston stated firmly. "I met her at a business mixer last month, and we had a one-night stand that was horrible. I'm actually surprised to see her here."

"She's a real estate associate of mine," Broderick said. "I wasn't aware you two knew each other."

"Well, I'm not trying to relive that awful night.

In fact, I need to respond to her text message right now before she gets the wrong impression and then block her number to prevent any more inappropriate pictures. I thought she took the hint when I never called her back about having Thanksgiving dinner with her family."

Braxton pressed his hand to Preston's forehead and then his cheek. "Are you feeling alright? Do you have a fever? Where is John Preston Chase III, and who are you? I don't recognize this man right here," he joked and shook Preston by the shoulders. "Come out, Prez."

Preston laughed. "Man, stop playing. I'm just not interested."

"Well, you were just staring the woman down before she strutted out the room, and you have a slew of pictures of other women on your phone in all kinds of interesting poses and positions."

"Yes, you used to drool over them, Braxton," Preston said sarcastically. "Didn't you have pictures in your phone as well, Mr. Jazz Pianist?"

"That was before Elle, but not anymore…well, unless you the count the ones that she sends me."

"Whatever, Brax. You were drooling, but now it's time to erase that photo album." He pushed the button that deleted the entire album on his phone and in the virtual cloud. Those women did absolutely nothing for him anymore. He was elated that he'd finally found a woman who cared for him and not how much money he could spend lavishing her with materialistic things. No one tugged at his heart like Blythe, and he couldn't wait to announce that she was all his. He figured the night of the Winter Wonderland would be perfect.

"Wow. I've seen it all. Is everything okay? Is there something you need to tell me and Broderick? You aren't dying, are you?"

Preston chuckled. "Relax, cuz… I'm fine. I'm just…in a good place, and there are some things forthcoming, but now isn't the time to discuss it."

"You're in love," Broderick stated matter-of-factly. "I know the signs, plus Tiffani was all giddy the other day about you having someone special in your life. Why didn't you bring her? We'd love to meet the woman who has you deleting your collection of pictures from your cell phone."

"And the cloud," Preston added.

Braxton chimed in. "If you deleted them from the cloud, you must really be serious about this girl."

"You two are hilarious. The world hasn't ended, and you'll meet her in due time, gentlemen. I'm going to go mingle a bit and perhaps have some dessert." *And by dessert, I mean Blythe Ventura à la mode.*

Strolling back inside the great room, he slid out his cell phone and typed a message to Blythe, who was chatting with Syd by the Christmas tree.

Meet me in the main laundry room on the terrace level in ten minutes.

With pleasure. Make it five minutes.

Even better, baby girl.

Preston slipped out unseen and made his way to the back hallway and down the stairs that led to the laundry room the housekeeper used. He figured no one would trek down there tonight. Blythe arrived a few moments later, but the saucy smile that he was expecting to see was turned upside down. She closed the door but didn't move toward him as her chest rose and fell, and he swore he saw steam coming from her head.

"What's wrong, baby girl?"

"Wow, what's wrong? Where should I begin?" she asked in a disdainful tone.

"Um…what's this about?" he questioned in a guarded manner. He couldn't figure out why she'd be upset with him.

"So, how long did you intend to play this game with me?"

Confusement filled him and his chest tightened as he strolled over to her, but she held her hand up to halt him.

"Don't come near me, you lying bastard," she yelled through clenched teeth. "I know about you and big-boobed Marissa."

"Oh, yeah, we used to kick it," he answered nonchalantly. "We had a one-night stand that wasn't very memorable, but that's it." Now he knew what the women were discussing at the table. If he'd known Marissa would be present at the party, he would've given Blythe a heads-up.

"Yes, just last month, and, apparently, tonight after the party. You're still juggling women, but you can drop this one. I *will not* be a part of some harem."

"What are you talking about? I'm not meeting her after the party, babe. That's not true."

She twisted her lips to the side as if she knew more to the story. "Oh, so she didn't send you naked pictures with an invite that you accepted?"

He chuckled and slid out his cell phone.

"Are you seriously laughing? This isn't funny." She opened the door, but he reached out and shut it.

"Wait, woman, before you start jumping to irrational conclusions." Handing her his cell phone, he opened the last text message he sent to Marissa and read it aloud while pointing to the words on the screen.

"'That's not going to happen tonight, or any other night, for that matter. I'm seeing someone, and even if I wasn't, I still wouldn't come.'" He took the phone back and ran a tender hand across her face that was filled with puzzlement. "That was my response before I blocked her number so I wouldn't receive any more text messages or phone calls from her. I'm not seeing Marissa or anyone else, sweetheart. Only you. Trust me, you're all the woman I need or can handle."

She sighed in relief and stepped back. "Prez... I'm sorry I jumped to conclusions, but... I..."

"No need to apologize. My past is quite scandalous in some areas. I figured something like this could happen, but not so soon."

"Yes, I'm fully aware of your past. It's just… well… I've been through this before, and I guess I thought I was living it again. Are there any other women here I need to know about?"

"No. Most of the women I've dated aren't close to my family. The only reason Marissa is here is that she and her dad own a real estate company that Broderick has done business with. You don't need to worry about her or anyone else. I'm tired of juggling. I think I was doing so because I hadn't found the one soul mate my heart craved." He drew her to him and lifted her chin up so he could have full eye contact with her. "Apparently you've been in front of me this entire time. I don't want or need anyone else. You fulfill me in ways I can't explain because I've never felt like this before you, Blythe. I'm falling in love with you."

She released the prettiest smile he'd ever seen on a woman.

A single tear trickled down her face. "I'm falling in love with you, too."

Preston nearly fell off balance at her words. He'd had women tell him that before, but with Blythe, they took on new meaning because he felt the same way.

He brushed his lips against hers. He never grew tired of kissing her luscious lips. Kissing women he knew weren't going to last long in relationships with him had never been on his list of foreplay. Sure, he'd kiss them for a second before getting down to business, but with Blythe, he wanted to savor her, taste her lips and make them and her body quiver with pleasure from being with him. She was all his and he was all hers. His heart had never truly belonged to a woman, but now it beat her name. She'd written her name all over it in her beautiful calligraphy.

She sighed sweetly against him, ran her hand up his cheek to his hair and massaged his head in a sensual manner that charged an electric current to jolt through him. Blythe was driving him crazy with passion, and he wanted her in that very instant. Originally he'd invited her down to the laundry room only to sneak in some kisses for a few minutes in private because he couldn't shake how seductive and exquisite she was in the red dress. He figured it would tide him over until later on. However, now he yearned to strip off her clothes and feel her warm brown-sugar skin next to him. He ached to be wrapped up tight in her embrace. He needed to remind her that she was the only one for him. Any other woman was a faint memory he never wanted to think about again. And he hadn't since he'd been with her.

Blythe released a sultry smize as he backed her up against the wall. His lips left hers and found their way to the side of her neck, which elicited the most breathtaking moans and trembles from her. He loved driving her insane. Loved hearing her pant his name in her raspy voice. She clutched his shoulders and arched her neck back as he bestowed deep licks to her skin over and over.

"Prez...baby...that feels so wonderful," she panted, holding on to his jacket lapels and pulling him even closer to him.

He sought to run his tongue over every inch of her body just to elicit the glorious sounds she made. Trailing his lips to the other side of her neck, he continued the sweet torture on her. He tried not to suck too hard for fear of leaving a mark, but the more she purred and gyrated her hips against his manhood, the more that idea seemed like a vague memory.

"Prez...uh...yes...baby, just like that." Her hand traveled to his belt buckle and began to unfasten it along with his pants. Her fingers moved to the top of his silk boxers and down into them as she ran her hand hard up and down the length of him. He could barely stand up or think straight as a powerful groan emerged from his throat. He was supposed to be driving her crazy. He was supposed to be in control, but with Blythe, she controlled everything and he didn't mind at all. It only made him need her more.

"That's what you want?" he asked gruffly, running his hand down her side until he reached the slit of her dress and slid his hand around to her bare bottom. Clenching it, he was glad she was wearing a thong. He slipped a finger inside her, and for a moment, she stopped stroking and tightened her grasp around him as she gasped and moaned, long and joyful.

"Ah…my…goodness… Prez…" she whimpered, trying to catch her breath. "Mmm… Prez…"

"So, this is what you want?" he asked with his lips against hers as he entered her with another finger, causing her to squirm and whisper his name.

"That…and so much…um…more. Damn, baby. Do you…um…shoot…ever let up? I can't breathe."

"I'll do whatever you want, baby girl."

"I know you will. That's why I can't get enough of you."

She began to undo the buttons of his tuxedo jacket and flung it off of him and to the floor, followed by his bow tie. Pushing him playfully away from her, she rested heated eyes on him in an intense, erotic stare that made him very elated to be in her presence. Reaching under her dress, she eased out of her panties and tossed them to him. He placed the lacy material in his shirt pocket. "You're not getting them back," he teased, patting his pocket.

"Whatever. The pants, too," she demanded.

"Slow down, woman. I'm getting there." Preston reached around to his back pocket and pulled out his wallet, hoping like hell he an emergency condom in there. When he saw the gold foil sticking out among a couple of hundred-dollar bills, he sighed in relief. His willpower was strong, but not around her. He didn't think he could wait until the party was over to jet back to his house. He had to have her now.

"Hurry the hell up."

"Yes, ma'am," he replied with a salute.

He did as instructed. He stepped out of his shoes, took off his pants along with the boxers and walked toward her when she curved her finger to him in a come-here gesture and mouthed it at the same time. She snatched the wrapper, opened it and rolled the condom on him. Lifting her leg around his waist, he rested his eyes directly on hers and plunged deep into her with one fluid stroke, which released a loud pant from her. Her muscles clenched firm around his penis, causing him to hammer into her harder and faster. Even though they were nowhere near the party and he could faintly hear the music, he was concerned that Blythe was becoming louder with every single thrust, and he muffled her blissful cries with his mouth. But that only caused him to shudder with being joined with her in every way.

He restrained himself. He wasn't ready yet to climax, even though this could only be a quickie, which he hated. He was sure people were searching for them, because he could distantly hear both of their cell phones vibrating. However, this was going to be the best quickie ever, just to tide them over until they made it back to his loft.

Lifting her up on him, he carried her to one of the folding tables, set her on her down and turned her body around. Slapping her bottom playfully, he bent her over and plunged in again, then didn't move. He settled his hands on her butt and clasped it. She glanced over her shoulder with a raised eyebrow as he began to move in and out of her with long, slow and deep strokes, over and over. She spread her arms out on the table and held on to the edge of it in front of her. Her pleasured moans started to explode once more, and he leaned over to her ear.

"Shh, baby. I know it feels good."

"So good, Prez," she whispered. "Mmm…don't stop, babe." Her voice became loud again, and she giggled. "Sorry. I'm trying…mmm…so hard not… to scream."

"We have to be quiet," he reminded her. "Use your inside voice."

"I can't help it." She trembled and tried to muffle her sounds.

"Don't worry. You can scream and curse as loud as you want later on at my place."

"Mmm…who says I'm coming over?" she asked with a teasing wink as she glanced at him over her shoulder.

He popped her bottom again and drove all the way into her. "Me." He sucked the side of her neck hard as the waves of satisfaction began to overtake him. Like her, he was trying his damnedest to stay quiet, but it was becoming impossible.

Preston continued his thrusts, which turned from slow and deep to fast and deep as the orgasm that neared blasted through his veins. He let out a slew of curse words and terms of endearment mixed in on the side of her neck as he shuddered controllably against her. Holding her tightly, he bucked when the aftershock hit him and breathed out as quietly as possible. She was right. That was hard to do.

"I'm not the only one," Blythe sang with a chuckle. "Sounds like someone is having problems keeping quiet, too."

"You do things to me I can't even explain, baby girl." He drew her to him, and she fell limp in his arms as a pleased smile rested on her face. "You're one in a million."

"Mmm…how sweet. I just hope I can walk back up the stairs in these heels. I'm pooped."

"You can take the elevator, but don't get too pooped. Round two…maybe even three later on."

"Oh… I'll be ready."

Later on that night, after round two, Preston held her close to him in his bed as she slept peacefully in his arms. Her naked body against his, warm and sated, was the perfect way to fall asleep. He'd never realized falling in love could be so special. Making love to a woman was far different than having sex or effing her. It was an exhilarating high. A rush of passion that raced through him, knowing that she was all his in mind, body, heart and soul. He remembered Braxton explaining that to him once. Now Preston understood fully what his cousin meant, and he wasn't ever going to let her go.

Chapter 9

"Hey, *chica*," Blythe said, entering Tiffani's bakery after the Tuesday morning rush. "Have any dark chocolate sweet treats? Doesn't matter what it is. I just need something to pep me up. I was up late finishing the last mural." *And I got up early for a morning love session with Preston, who surprised me with breakfast at my house.*

"I sure do." Tiffani smiled pleasantly. She opened the display case and pulled out two cream cheese brownies and placed them on a napkin. "Gluten-free, just how you like them. Are you going to eat here? I'd love to chat with you if you have time."

Blythe sat at the counter and inhaled the delicious smell. "I have some time before my first session at noon. I haven't seen you since the party. How are you?"

"I'm good and well-rested. Just needed to relax after having five hundred people in my home, so Broderick and I jetted off to our private island for a few days for some relaxation and fun without KJ and his dog. They stayed with his paternal grandparents."

"Cool. The party was awesome. I need Chef Crenshaw's recipes for the seared lamb and roasted brussels sprouts. Oh, and the shrimp quiche." She hadn't tasted the last dish, but Preston had raved about it, so she figured she'd make it for him one day.

"I'll have him email them to you. And how are you? All set with the Winter Wonderland project?"

"Oh, yeah. Everything is ready. Five more days! The committee is prepared and excited."

"I have a ton of cupcakes to bake, too." Tiffani glanced up as her assistant Kendall walked into the shop from the kitchen. "Kendall, can you watch the front for a few minutes? I need to go back to my office with Blythe."

"Sure, Boss," Kendall answered, as she settled in behind the counter.

Blythe grabbed her brownies and wondered why Tiffani wanted to talk in private. She hoped everything was okay with her best friend. Once they were settled on the couch, Tiffani turned to her with a wide smile that she was trying to suppress.

"What, girl? You have some great news to tell me?" Blythe asked as Tiffani could hardly contain herself. She was giddy and jumpy, which meant it was either good news or some gossip about one of the other store owners in the shopping center. Or perhaps she was pregnant. Tiffani had mentioned recently she wanted to start trying again soon.

Tiffani shook her head. "Nooo, I think *you* have some great news to share with *me*."

Blythe pondered for a moment. "Mmm…no… I don't think so." She shook her head as innocently as possible, but she had a feeling that Tiffani knew her secret. But how? She and Preston had agreed they'd tell Tiffani together when the time was right.

Tiffani smacked her lips and cut her eyes playfully at Blythe. "Now, girl, we've been best friends for almost two years, and I know when something is up with you. I wasn't sure exactly what it was until I was perusing the camera monitors last night, searching for the party footage. One of my guests lost an emerald earring, and I was trying to find her with it on and to see when it fell off. Well, I did, and I was able to return it to her this morning."

Blythe's heart sank, and a wave of panic washed over her body. A trickle of nervous sweat formed at the nape of her neck. She prayed with all her might that Tiffani wasn't about to say that she saw Preston and her in the laundry room doing the wild thang on the folding table.

Tiffani cleared her throat before continuing, wearing a wicked smirk. "But I also saw you and my brother in the main laundry room, arguing about what, I don't know, because there's no sound, thank goodness. The next scene I saw, you two were getting busy on the wall. I stopped watching because—well, he *is* my brother, but I saved the DVD just in case you want it for your personal library. It's locked in my desk drawer."

"Um…see…what had happened was…" she started sarcastically. "Prez and I are…well…"

"Uh-huh…go ahead and explain it to me, please." Tiffani bounced up on the couch and tucked her legs underneath.

Blythe tried to suppress the embarrassment that was forming. "How much of the wall action did you see?" Perhaps there was a way to not divulge everything just yet.

"I stopped it when you took your panties off and tossed them to him, even though before that, I was watching through my fingers."

"Oh…" she said in complete mortification.

"Now I know why I couldn't find either of you for thirty minutes, but I never thought about you two being somewhere together. However, that would explain the bite on your neck that you said must've come from an insect when you'd stepped outside to take a phone call. But now I know it was a human bite, not a bug bite. And honestly, I thought Prez was somewhere in my house doing the nasty with Marissa, but she left rather early that evening. I am going to assume that he's the reason you've been glowing lately, and that you're the special lady he said I would adore…which I do, by the way."

"I'd better be… I mean, yes I am," Blythe answered.

Tiffani put her hand up to her face as tears welled up in her eyes. "Ah…so now we're going to be best friends and sisters? I'm so excited." She grabbed Blythe's hands. "This is so surreal. Now all the Chases are in love. I told you miracles happen around Christmas."

"Slow down, Tiff. We just started seeing each other," she reminded her. "We're still in the beginning stages."

"But you've known him for a year, and you told me that the next man you had sex with would be the one you married. I'm assuming you've had sex, considering you tossed your panties at him."

"Yes, Tiffani, we have, and I hope that we are together forever, but we're still taking it one day at a time. We haven't even told anyone we're seeing each other, even though I think the committee suspects it. Now that you know, I guess we can start telling people we're a couple."

"But why didn't you tell me? I'm your best friend. I've secretly wanted you two together since you first met. My brother was smitten with you. I was there. I know him and I know you. I figured one day both of you would wake up and smell the coffee. You're perfect for each other, and maybe getting together when you first met would've been disastrous because

Preston wasn't ready for a real relationship. Now he's glowing and happy and it's all because of you, and I can't stop smiling. I wanted to call you last night, but Broderick suggested I calm down my excitement first. I was way too giddy to talk."

"I agree, when we met would not have been the right time, but it is now. I didn't want to tell you or anybody just in case things didn't work out. I have to admit, I've been attracted to him since last year, but not enough to act on it. But after spending time with him working on the project and getting to know the kind of man Preston truly is and not the party playboy, I decided to take a chance, and I'm glad I did. Preston is a great guy."

"Ah…how sweet. I'm so elated for you both."

"Me, too. I have no regrets." She glanced at her watch. "I need to go. I have to prepare for a paint party."

The ladies stood and headed toward the door, but Blythe stopped as she remembered something and turned to Tiffani.

"Tiff, um…so you really have the DVD in your drawer?"

"Oh, yeah," Tiffani answered, jetting to her desk and unlocking it. She pulled out a DVD case and handed it over to Blythe. "You know I got you covered, girl!"

Blythe lay on her favorite chaise lounge in front of a roaring fire at Preston's loft. She played a video game he wanted feedback for on his cell phone while he took Hope for a walk. She was comfortable, happy and content with her life. Tiffani was right, because miracles did happen at Christmas. Never in her wildest imagination did she think this time last year that she'd be chilling in Preston Chase's loft, sipping hot chocolate, playing video games and waiting for him to return so they could cuddle and relax by the fireplace. She couldn't believe she'd fallen for him in such a short period of time, but in her heart she knew she'd always cared for him. The fear of being hurt again had been the culprit holding her back, because in some ways he reminded her of her ex, who was a player. Now that everyone in his immediate family knew they were a couple and were elated for them, she was even happier about her decision to date him.

The past few days had been hectic, preparing for the Winter Wonderland, and last-minute changes on Preston's part had swamped his time. She'd spent the day with Sasha, Megan and other volunteers wrapping tons of presents for the children and placing them around the Christmas trees. She was due back tomorrow to finish up, and the following day would be the big event. Blythe could hardly believe it was happening and couldn't wait to see Preston's vision for the children come to life.

A beep and a flash of words on the cell phone screen interrupted the game. Frowning because she was just about to advance to the next level after five tries, she read a text message from Marissa Stewart. Nausea arose in her throat as she read the short message in her head.

Thank you for last night, Prez. ☺

Last night? What did Marissa mean, *last night*? And why was there a smiley face? Blythe's heart began to race at one hundred miles per hour as the cell phone burned in her hands. Her breathing became unhinged as she racked her brain trying to remember everything Preston said he did *last night*, and somehow Marissa's name never came out of his mouth.

Last night he did a final walk-through at the Winter Wonderland venue with Devin and Jonathan. She'd wanted to be there, but she had two paint parties back to back, and the last one didn't end until after midnight because it was a bachelorette party. He was supposed to come over to her house but didn't because he was hanging out with Braxton at his jazz club. Their cousins Sean and Cannon Arrington were in town from Memphis with their families for Christmas.

Was that one big lie? Had Prez actually gone over to Marissa's after all? Blythe looked at the phone again. No more text messages had come through, but the same one stared at her in big, bold letters along with that dang smiley face. It felt like a slap across her face as tears began to sting her cheeks. Tossing the phone to his chaise lounge, she stood as the elevator doors opened and Hope ran straight to her mat by the fire. She crossed her arms over her chest and waited impatiently for him to come around the corner.

"Babe, you want to watch our hot, steamy video again?" Preston yelled out, placing the dog leash back on the hook. "Your facial expressions when I had you bent over and couldn't see you were erotic as hell." He strolled toward her wearing a devilish smile that quickly faded away. "Baby girl, what's wrong? Why are you crying? Somebody died?" He reached for her, but she backed up as confusion filled his face.

"Yes…we did. Our relationship is dead."

His forehead scrunched and he stepped toward her. "Wait…what are you talking about? I was only walking the dog for, like, twenty minutes. What the hell happened while I was gone?"

"Check your cell phone," she demanded, pointing to it. "You have a text message."

The puzzlement was erased from his face and was replaced with concern while he exhaled as if there was nothing truly wrong. Stepping toward her, he placed his hands on her shoulders and said calmly, "Blythe, the women I've dated may call me sometimes for whatever reason, and they don't know I'm in a relationship. If someone is asking to go out or something, it's no big deal. I promise. Would you like me to call all of them? It may take a while, but I'll do it."

Moving back, she placed her hands on her hips. "Marissa knows you're in a relationship, and if I remember correctly, you said you blocked her number at the party after she sent you the inappropriate pictures."

Walking away from her, he swiped the cell phone from the chaise and mumbled under his breath as he read the message.

"Okay, so this could look bad, but it's really not." He waved his hands in front of him. "I've done nothing wrong. You know I haven't."

"Oh, really?" She wiped her tears away. *Why the hell am I crying in front of him? He deserves no tears from me.* She had to stay strong right now. She could cry later at home.

"Please explain this one to me, but before you do, remember I dated a player just like you. There were so many red flags being thrown at me, you'd think I was a batter on a baseball team. But I was young, immature and naive, thinking that I was the only one and that he loved me when he didn't. I was caught up because he was handsome not realizing until it was too late that I was just a part of a freaking harem. Now I know exactly what to look for before it's too late. But go ahead and throw your best lie out there. I'm dying to hear all about *last night.*"

He chuckled, which annoyed her to the fullest. Her ex used to the do the same crap when he was caught in a lie. It was the similar nervous laugh that her ex used to give himself time to figure out how to weasel his way out of whatever he'd done to get caught.

"Last night, I met my cousins at the jazz club, which you are fully aware of because I called you before we went in. Marissa was there and tipsy as hell. She tried to persuade me to go home with her to have sex, but I told her no. I reminded her that I was in a relationship, and there was nothing she could do to convince me. She became irate and made a scene in the middle of the lobby area in front of the people waiting in line to get in. Braxton called security, and she attempted to leave but was stumbling and fell at one point.

"I snatched her keys from her because she was in no condition to drive. I drove her home in her car with Sean following us in my car. We made sure she got in safely, she fell asleep on the couch and we left. That's it. That's why she's thanking me. I unblocked her number this morning to call and check on her. She was really wasted. She didn't answer, but I left a voice mail, so I guess she's sending a text message now. I haven't heard from her all day."

Blythe shook her head back and forth. "I don't believe any of the story you just told me except that you took her home."

"What?" he yelled loudly, waking Hope, who jetted over and lay next to his feet. "You're kidding me, right? I just told you the truth."

"If you say so." She shrugged. "I've never seen anyone get wasted at Braxton's club. His bartenders know when to cut people off. It's not that kind of establishment."

"Blythe, I don't know what else you want me to do or say. I'm not lying to you. I have no reason to lie to you."

"Okay, so, if nothing happened, why didn't you tell me this sooner? Like, when I asked."

"I didn't see the need to," he answered calmly as if it wasn't a big deal. "Am I supposed to tell you every single little thing that goes on in my life?"

"I asked you about last night earlier today. You said you had a blast catching up with your cousins, but at no time did you mention leaving the club to take Marissa home."

"Again, I didn't see the point. She doesn't live far from the club. We were back in thirty minutes, and we continued our evening. It wasn't a big deal, even though you're making it one."

"You were supposed to come over last night."

"It was late by the time we left. Hell, the club was closed when we finally left. We sat around, smoked cigars, drank bourbon and listened to Braxton play the piano until four in the morning, which I told you about," he retorted through gritted teeth. "I haven't lied to you."

"Sooo…you didn't see the need to tell me you took

home one of your exes in the middle of your alleged grand time with your cousins?"

"She's not an ex. We had a one-night stand. That's it, but I've done nothing wrong to you, Blythe. I was just being polite. The woman was drunk and I wanted her out of my cousin's establishment. That's it."

She stared at him in disbelief. She wanted to believe him, and in a way, she did, but at the same time she didn't understand why he couldn't be honest in the first place. Why had he kept it from her?

"You could've told me," she said quietly.

"It was no big deal."

"Mmm-hmm...okay, if you say so."

Leaving the sitting area, she headed down the hall to the master bedroom and grabbed her rolling overnight suitcase along with her coat and purse. When she returned, she found him seated on the chaise with Hope at his feet. He looked up when she approached, and a scowl reached his face as he glanced at her belongings.

"Where are you going?" he asked, striding to her and blocking her path.

"Home." She moved around him, but he sidestepped and stood in front of her once more. Groaning, she tried to push through. The tears needed to fall again, but they weren't going to fall in front of him. She couldn't believe this was happening.

He held his hands up. "Wait...why?" he asked with frustration. "It's late."

Looking past him, she inhaled and spoke as calmly as possible. "I want to be alone right now."

"I understand you're upset with me. And that's fine. You're entitled to be mad if you choose to be, but you don't have to leave, baby girl. There are plenty of rooms. I'll sleep in the guest room."

"No, I mean at my own home. Away from you."

Looking taken aback, he stepped away from her. "You can't seriously be mad at me," he stated in a defensive tone. "I was trying to protect your feelings, that's all, and to avoid this type of confrontation, because again, it's no big deal. Nothing happened and you know nothing happened. I wouldn't do that to you, Blythe."

"I'm not mad at you. I'm upset with me for getting involved with you, knowing you have a promiscuous past. I promised myself never to get involved with another pretty boy playboy, and what did I do?" she asked sarcastically. "I can't do this again. I have to be able to trust you."

"I'm not him."

"You're just alike. For whatever reason, I tend to attract your kind."

"Blythe, what is your problem? I didn't tell you for the simple fact that I wanted to avoid this conversation. I know you weren't thrilled with hearing her tell your group at the party about the naked pictures and the invite I declined. You saw the text message I sent her."

"You should've been honest with me and told me. It's like you hid it because you felt guilty about it. It's almost like you cheated on me."

He wiped his hands down his face and breathed out. He was silent for a minute before he began to speak in a calm but firm manner.

"I'm not going to argue with you over something trivial. I didn't cheat on you, and I did nothing inappropriate. If you think withholding information to protect your heart is wrong, then fine. I was wrong. If I wanted to hide something from you, do you think I would let you use my cell phone to play a game? I gave you the freaking pass code to it." His voice rose and continued to do so. "Did any other female call or text while you were playing? I'll answer that for you. No. You wanna know why? Because they can't. Because I went through and blocked all their numbers. They can't call or text me unless it's from a number that I don't have. You want to know why I blocked them? Because I'm with you. I don't want them. Never did."

Blythe listened to him, but there was something still nagging at her heart. She'd gone through this before. She'd believed and forgiven her ex over something very similar, only to find out he'd lied, and it wasn't just once. She thought she'd left all of that in her twenties. Now, at thirty, this crap was resurfacing, and she blamed no one but herself.

"I need time to think," she whispered. "And I can't do it here."

"Fine, you want to leave?" He stepped out of her way and pointed to the elevator. "Go, because I'm not going to argue with you over something so petty."

Taken aback, she almost had a half a mind to curse him out for talking to her like that. Arguments were never her forte, and she didn't want to end up saying the wrong thing and make matters worse.

"Good night," she said.

He strolled over to the elevator and pushed the button to open the doors. "Good night."

After Blythe left, Preston plopped on his chaise lounge and stared up at the painting. Letting out a deep sigh, he rehashed their argument in his head. He truly didn't understand why she was upset with him. He had told the freaking truth. Isn't that what every woman wanted? The truth? True, he didn't disclose the information upfront but he honestly didn't see the need to. He thought he was doing the honorable thing by making sure Marissa got home safely. He'd figured withholding what happened from Blythe would be best because he didn't want her upset or to think he was seeing Marissa.

Glancing at pouting Hope on her mat in front of him, he let out a nervous chuckle as the dog stood and nudged his hand. "Girl, I think I've messed up."

Sliding off the chaise, he made his way to the

game room with Hope by his side. Grabbing a pool stick from the wall, he trekked over to the pool table, lifted the rack that contained the balls and broke them. Watching them go in different directions, only one landed in the pocket. He tossed the stick on the table and ran his hands down his face. Preston couldn't believe this was happening. He had finally found the one woman he'd searched for all his life only to let her walk out the door and possibly out of his life because his scandalous past had finally caught up with him.

Preston hated the sad and hurt expression on her face. He hated that he'd caused it and didn't do anything to comfort her. Even if she did believe him the fact that he'd withheld something that she'd deemed important hadn't sat well with her. He'd been a total jerk to Blythe, and she didn't deserve to be treated that way.

He knew some of it had to do with her ex that had cheated and while she said she wasn't heartbroken, he could understand why she didn't exactly trust him either. But Blythe was different from every other woman he'd dated and the difference was he'd fallen in love with her. This wasn't the first time he argued with a woman over another woman. In those instances, he shrugged it off because he simply didn't care. However, this time he did and now he felt like crap. His heart clenched at the thought of this being the end all because of his male ego standing in the way. All because he couldn't admit to her at that moment he was wrong. Instead, he let her walk out. Perhaps he should've chased after her, but she was too upset and he'd learned from his father that sometimes it's best to give a woman her space to cool down or it could make matters worse.

Plopping on the leather sectional, Hope joined him and stared up at him with sad eyes. He ruffled the dog's head and then closed his eyes as he reminisced on the good times he'd shared with Blythe. She had been a breath of fresh air in his life, and he wasn't about to let her get away.

Chapter 10

"Everything is perfect. Just how Preston wanted it," Sasha said to Blythe and Tiffani as the ladies strolled around the Winter Wonderland event.

The overly excited children played arcade games, waited in line to see Santa Claus, played with the animals in the petting zoo and rode the train and the merry-go-round. There were more children outside at the ice-skating rink and the Ferris wheel or sledding on the fake snow hills. Songs from the cartoon *A Charlie Brown Christmas*, performed by Braxton and his jazz band, lent a festive atmosphere. Children and their parents lined up for carnival-type foods and took pictures in one of the four photo booths. Blythe tried to tear her eyes away from the third booth as images of Preston and her filled her head.

"I'm so glad you all were available to help him make it come alive," Tiffani said with pride. "The children are having a blast. I don't think I've seen so many overjoyed faces."

Blythe nodded her head. "Indeed, they are. It's truly a joyous occasion."

Sasha beamed bright as Devin approached. "Ready for the Ferris wheel, babe?" she asked as he grabbed her to him and kissed her tenderly on the lips. "I guess that's a yes. Bye, ladies." Giggling, she skipped off hand in hand with her husband.

Tiffani followed Blythe to her art station, where her session was to begin in a few moments. She knew her best friend wanted to say something. It was written all over her face. For the past two days, Blythe had managed to avoid Preston except for a group conference call with the committee members about last-minute changes for the event. He'd sent a bouquet of yellow roses to her studio and another one to her home with a note that simply read, "I'm not going anywhere. Let me know when you're ready to talk." However, she wasn't sure she was ready to talk or to see Preston. It took every ounce of strength to attend the event tonight, but she wasn't there for him. She was there for the children.

Blythe had played the scenario over and over in her mind, and while she had probably overreacted, she could admit to herself that she was scared.

Maybe she'd gone into their relationship too soon. Maybe she shouldn't have slept with him so soon, even though she still didn't regret it. The feelings she had for Preston were real, but she felt the need to protect her heart. She missed him and was nervous as hell about seeing him tonight. Luckily he was so busy with the event and greeting the children, he'd managed to stay out of her sight except once, but she ducked out of his vision before he saw her.

When she arrived at the art station, on her table was another bouquet of yellow roses that hadn't been there twenty minutes ago. Sighing, she slid the card from its holder and read it. "I miss you, baby girl. Still here."

"I see my brother isn't giving up," Tiffani said, running her fingers along the roses and smelling them. "This is the third bunch, right?"

Blythe breathed out and slipped on her smock. "It's not that I don't believe him. It's that I just wish he'd told me up front. We're adults. There's no reason to hide anything from me. It makes me think otherwise. That's all."

Tiffani pressed her lips together and tapped her fingers on the table.

Blythe laughed at her friend's determination for the past few days to stay mum on the matter even though she could sense it was hard to do. "Go ahead. You have the floor," she said, bowing her head toward Tiffani.

Tiffani exhaled and wiped her hand across her forehead. "Whew, thank you. Well, I've promised you both I'd stay out of it. I will say I've never witnessed Preston this upset over possibly losing a woman. Sean and Cannon stopped by the bakery earlier today. Sean said that they took Marissa home and there was no hanky-panky. But I know that's not your issue. It's a trust thing and I understand. I know my brother and his past. I know all of his dirt. I've met a lot of his women and I know he hasn't always been honest, faithful or trustworthy. He's no saint. Heck, you knew half of his dirt thanks to me, but you trusted in your soul that he was a good guy and he had a heart."

Blythe nodded her head in silence. He definitely had a heart. Just observing all of the children and their parents' smiling faces signified that.

"Thank you, Tiffani, and I know you're trying your best to stay out of it, but I appreciate the information and all of the chocolate goodies you gave me yesterday. Chocolate will make anything seem halfway better."

Tiffani hugged her tight. "You're my best friend and sister regardless of whether or not you're with my brother. I just want you happy either way," she said sincerely, squeezing Blythe's hands. "You're still family."

"Thank you."

"Alright, I see you have some kiddies showing up to paint. I'm going to go check on KJ. He's probably still outside snow sledding with his friends, and my cupcake decorating class starts soon. He volunteered since he loves to claim he's part owner of Sweet Treats."

"Girl, he is not leaving snow sledding anytime soon. It rarely snows here in Atlanta."

"I know, right? I'll let him stay out there. See you in a bit."

Once her paint session was underway, Blythe was so engrossed and having so much fun with the children painting winter scenes that she didn't realize Preston was standing in the back, chatting with some of the parents. When she glanced up, their eyes met briefly before she placed her attention on a little girl who needed her assistance. However, every now and then her gaze would strain toward him and her heartbeat would speed up. Even though his focus was on the conversation, his stare was on her. He seemed tired but refreshed at the same time. He was in his element with the children he cared so much about. She had to admit she was proud of him and everything he'd done to make the event magical. Despite not knowing which direction she was headed with him, Blythe couldn't deny the fact that he was an exemplary human being who had brightened so many little lives that evening. It was one of the reasons she fell for him in the first place. She prayed they could move past this.

After the session ended and the children left, Preston strolled over to her.

"Need some help cleaning up?" he asked, placing the paintbrushes in a huge can of clean water that sat in the middle of the supply table. "I know your next session begins in a few."

"Sure." She left him with the paintbrushes and began to strip the tables of the butcher paper to replace it with more. They worked in heavy, annoying silence until she had everything set up again. He was so close in the small space allotted for her station. His sultry, woodsy cologne outweighed the paint fumes and she tried not to breathe it in. The notes from his cologne mixed in with his own scent always set her body on rage, and the nearness of him swept a storm of desire through her veins. But this was not the time or place to discuss anything or to be hot and bothered.

"The kids are enjoying themselves. You've done an outstanding job," she complimented him.

Tilting his head, he looked at her as if he was shocked she'd spoken to him. "Thank you, but all of this couldn't have been done without you and the committee's hard work. The entire team stepped up to the plate. I came in here this afternoon alone before any of you arrived, and I was in awe. I was speechless. It's beautiful, and even more beautiful now that the children are here having the best time of their lives, so thank you for helping me make it possible."

"You're very welcome, but this is all *you*. Your vision. Your kind heart loving and giving back so unselfishly. Most people want to be at home with their loved ones drinking hot chocolate and wrapping gifts on Christmas Eve, not doing this. Not sacrificing so much of your time and money. I know you don't care about the money part because at the end of the day you just want to give the children some joy and hope for Christmas. You've been in their shoes. You've experienced the pain they've suffered at such a young age. You have shown these children so much love, and I know their parents are truly grateful for everything you've done and will continue to do. I spoke to a mother earlier and she went on and on about so many things you've done for the children's hospital and for her family. She mentioned how she'd quit her job because she refused to leave her daughter in the hospital and while her husband works, they could barely make ends meet. She said you paid their mortgage for a year until they got back on their feet. Another lady told me how her son's wish was to meet his favorite football player and you had set it up the very next day. So, no, I can't take credit for any of this. It is a wonderful experience, and I'm thankful to be a part of it. However, this is your vision, and I couldn't be more proud of you than I am now."

Her voice cracked and tears welled in her eyes, but she pushed them back when he stepped toward her.

"Blythe... I..."

She shook her head and looked past him to see two boys skip over to Preston.

"Mr. Preston," they both shouted at the same time.

Preston's face lit up even more as he turned around to the boys who bombarded him.

"Hey, Lionel and Scott." He scooped them up for a big hug. "You just got here?"

"Yeah, our mom got stuck in traffic," Lionel explained. "This is awesome. Thank you so much, Mr. Preston."

"No problem, son," Preston said. "What do you want to do first? Arcade games? See Santa Claus? The petting zoo?"

"Snow sledding and then the petting zoo," Lionel answered. "Oh, and the Ferris wheel."

"Are you coming with us?" Scott asked.

"For sure," Preston answered matter-of-factly. "Let's get some hot apple cider first."

"Cool, with whipped cream?" Lionel grabbed Preston's hand, followed by Scott, who held the other one.

"You bet. Lots of it, and with cinnamon," Preston said, glancing at Blythe over his shoulder. He mouthed "I love you" before the boys pulled him away. Two more boys approached them and joined the group, as well.

Blythe wiped her eyes and put on a happy face as her next group began to form, and for the following thirty minutes, they worked on their winter scenes. She was glad for the interruption because it kept her from focusing on what Preston said before he jetted off with the boys. However, once her session ended, the words *"I love you"* played in her head over and over like a broken record. He'd told her he was falling for her, but never with those three words. Her eyes perused the yellow roses once more, and she read the card again.

Afterward she joined Tiffani, who was finishing up her cupcake decorating session. For the next few hours until the event ended at midnight, the ladies walked around the venue, assisting where they were needed. She ran into Preston a couple more times. He was having fun with the children, playing games and taking pictures with them.

Once the last child left, Preston gathered all the committee members at the entrance of Santa's Village. He stood next to the mural of Hope as his assistants passed out glasses filled with champagne. Preston's eyes roamed over everyone and lingered on Blythe a little longer before clearing his throat.

"I don't even know where to begin. I guess I'll start from the beginning. When I first thought of doing the Winter Wonderful project, it was this summer, and I'd just found out that one of the children…" He stopped as his voice lowered and cracked. Breathing out, Preston started again. "This summer…um… Haley, one of the children at the hospital, had been out of remission for a year. She was rediagnosed with cancer, but this time it came back more aggressive, spreading to other organs, and unfortunately she died. Haley was only seven, and Christmas was her favorite holiday. The doctors pretty much said she had only a few more weeks, maybe months, but probably not. So we moved Christmas up for her and had a celebration in her hospital room because she was too weak to go to the playroom." He stopped again as tears rushed down his cheeks.

"She died a few days later, and it broke my heart and those of the children she'd befriended at the hospital. I knew then I wanted to do something special for them, and the wheels in my head began to turn with ideas. I wanted it to be memorable and extraordinary, out of this world, and thanks to all of you, it was. Someone told me earlier this evening that it was all me, but the truth is I couldn't have done this without all of you pitching in, sacrificing your time with your families and loved ones over the past month, putting this all together. On New Year's Eve, you know I'm having a big thank-you party in your honor, but I also have something else for each of you." He turned toward Linda.

Linda wiped her tears and patted Preston's face. "You know you're like a son to me and my husband. We're so proud of you." Then she turned to face the audience. "To show his appreciation, Preston is giving everyone an all-expenses-paid trip for you, significant others and your children to Hawaii for one week. It doesn't matter when you want to go. You'll just need to contact me so I can make the arrangements. I'll start the day after Christmas. You all have my contact information at work."

The committee members, including Blythe, clapped and cheered and thanked Preston, who was overwhelmed with emotion. They all raised their champagne glasses and toasted him.

Smiling, Preston raised his glass. "Thank you, and I'm raising my glass to toast all of you. You just don't know how much tonight meant to me, and I hope we can all do this again next year and the year after that."

Everyone clinked their glasses with the people they were standing next to. Blythe toasted hers with Tiffani and was surprised when the next glass she clinked was Preston's. She hadn't realized he'd made his way to her. Afterward everyone began to disperse and leave. Blythe walked with Tiffani as KJ went on and on about his evening and how his Uncle Preston said he could return the day after Christmas with his best friends to play once more before everything was taken down. Blythe hadn't realized how tired she was until she yawned and fumbled around in her purse for her keys.

"You're forgetting these."

Blythe halted in her tracks at the deep voice behind her. She turned to find Preston holding the vase of yellow roses. Tiffani squeezed her hand and winked at Preston before leaving them alone.

Great, is Tiffani really leaving me? "Oh... I didn't mean to forget them. I'm just tired from this evening. I'm exhausted, but not as exhausted as you, I'm sure. You've been with the children playing all the games and enjoying the rides like a big kid. I saw you on the merry-go-around."

He chuckled. "Yeah, but it was well worth it. They'll remember this evening for a long while. So will I. Can't wait until next year. It's going to be even bigger!"

"Is that even possible?" she questioned in a joking manner, because she knew with him it was very possible. "You look so tired, Prez. You'll probably sleep all day tomorrow."

He nodded his head with a sleepy smile. "Mmm... I suppose. It's Christmas tomorrow...in fact, it's Christmas now."

"Oh, yeah...it's after midnight." She continued walking with him by her side. "Merry Christmas," she said uneasily as they stopped at the door of the lobby and she remembered their plans for tomorrow.

A naughty smile formed across his face. "Merry Christmas to you, baby girl," he said, glancing up and then settled his smoldering gaze back on her. "You know where you're standing, right?"

She glanced up at the mistletoe as her breath caught in her throat. "I can run really fast to my car," she joked, tilting her body as if she was about to run.

"Doesn't matter." He shrugged, closing the gap between them. "I'd still catch you, either way. I'm sure you'd love the chase."

She shook her head. "You don't quit, do you?"

"I've told you before, when I want something, I go after it. Like the card with the roses said, I'm still here. You're not pushing me away that easily over a disagreement."

Setting the roses on the floor, he grabbed her to him and crashed his lips on hers in an untamed, fervent kiss. Pleasure soared through her body at the intensity and passion of his lips on hers. His hands ran down her sides and clenched her hips, bringing her closer to him. His body meshed with hers, and she could feel the hardness of his chest, his abs, his manhood and his thighs pressed against her in an erotic way. It was almost like they were one. She didn't feel his sweater or jeans against her. She felt the warmth of his skin radiate through her clothes and onto her skin. Their connection was strong. The protective and loving embrace he had her wrapped in was peaceful and serene. She was where she wanted and needed to be. She'd missed the hell out of him.

"I've missed you, woman. You know that?" he asked between kisses. "It's been two days and I've missed you like it's been twenty years."

"Me, too. Prez… I…feel like I need to apologize to you for act—"

He placed his finger over her lips. "Shh…don't say anything. Not tonight. It's been a long, overwhelming day, but tomorrow we'll talk. You aren't the one who needs to apologize. We'd originally made plans for Christmas before our disagreement, and I'd like to keep them since you're not going home to Brooklyn for the holidays. So, brunch at my place and dinner with my family at Megan's?" ·

"Yes, I'll be there, and I hate that we argued, too."

He stooped down and picked the roses up. "I'll walk you out."

Later on that night, as Blythe drifted off to sleep, she finally made her decision about Preston and her future with him.

Chapter 11

When Blythe strolled into Preston's home Christmas morning, she was in awe at the extravagant decorations. The fireplace was flanked with evergreen garlands and holly, three stockings were hanging from the mantel, and a huge Christmas tree with gold-and-silver ornaments stood proudly in the center of the main seating area, lit with white lights. There were other over-the-top decorations around the loft as well, and delicious aromas from the kitchen reached her nose.

Hope, who was adorned in reindeer antlers and jingle bells around her collar, rushed toward her with a rapidly wagging tail.

"Hey, pretty girl." Blythe set her belongings and

purse on the floor to hug the dog. "Are you really happy to see me, or you just want your peanut butter-flavored bone in the bag?" She ruffled the dog's fur. "I know you can smell it."

"*I'm* happy to see you," a low, sexy voice remarked in front of her. "*Very* happy."

A warm wave washed over her skin, and she glanced up to see Preston emerge from the kitchen and head toward them. Standing, she kept her hand on the dog's collar for support since she was still somewhat anxious about their upcoming conversation.

"Hi, Prez. Merry Christmas," she said nervously as everything she needed to say to him filled her head and was ready to rush out of her mouth.

"Merry Christmas, indeed." Yanking her by the waist to him, he dipped her and kissed her slowly on the lips. "I'm glad you're here. I thought you might not want to spend it with me." He raised her back up and held her in his embrace, swaying back and forth to the Christmas jazz playing through the speakers mounted throughout his home.

"No… I told you I would come. I want to spend Christmas with you, but…" She stopped as she thought about the elephant in the room.

"I know…" He caressed her face and stared at her with an apologetic expression. "We need to talk about what happened, and I want to start first."

"Okay. Let me put the cake in the fridge before I forget about it."

His eyebrow rose at the mention of the only dessert she knew how to make. "You brought the cake? It will go perfect with brunch. The caterers dropped everything off earlier."

Her eyes perused the living area. "And did they decorate, as well? It's immaculate in here. I wasn't expecting a mini Winter Wonderland. Is there snow somewhere, too?" she teased. "Are we going snow sledding?"

"No, babe. No snow, but I wanted something special for you. I know how much you love Christmas, and you aren't with your family this year. The same company that did the trees for last night's event did the decorations this morning. I just wanted it perfect for you."

"Well, it is. Thank you." She skipped over to the bags by the elevator with Hope on her heels. Blythe reached into one of them and gave Hope her present, and the dog darted off to her favorite spot in front of the fireplace and started to lick the bone.

"She's going to be busy all day, chomping on that huge thing," Preston remarked. "Thank you."

"No problem." She grabbed the box with the cake and made her way to the kitchen as she thought about everything she'd intended to say to him. She'd tossed and turned while mulling it over last night and thought about it some more during the drive to his home. However, since he wanted to go first, she'd hear him out. Setting the cake in the refrigerator, she turned to find him leaning on the island and staring at her intently. She assumed he wasn't the only one ready to discuss their argument.

Clasping her hand in his, he led her to their favorite spot in front of the fireplace. That's when she noticed there was a stocking for her, Preston and Hope. Their names were sewn on them. It reminded her of home in Brooklyn. Her mother would hang one for each of their family members, as well. Sitting down, she tucked her legs underneath her, grabbed one of the toss pillows from the back of the chaise and held on to it tightly. She thought Preston would join her or sit on the other chaise, but instead he stood and paced around for a few seconds before kneeling in front of her.

Exhaling, he reclasped his hands with hers and gave her full eye contact. "Blythe, I want to start by saying I'm sorry for not telling you that I took Marissa home. I'm sorry I don't have a reason other than the one I already gave. I know that sounds terrible, but just listen to me."

"Okay. I'll hear you out." *Because that's not exactly how I expected that to come out.*

"I have to admit that no other woman has held me accountable for anything like that before. I'm used to doing whatever I want and not having to answer to anyone, but that's no excuse. I wasn't intentionally trying to lie or hide anything from you. You're very special to me, baby girl, and your feelings are important to me. I've been going crazy at the notion of losing you over not understanding your feelings. I sincerely apologize for hurting you and being insensitive to the fact that you were hurting. I shouldn't have called the argument petty because it mattered to you and therefore it was a big deal. I truly hope you can accept my apology and forgive me for being a jackass."

Squeezing his hands, she let the sincerity and honesty of his words sink in before speaking.

Closing her eyes, she inhaled deeply. "Prez, I accept your apology. I shouldn't have overreacted. And I shouldn't have compared you to my ex. You're right. You're nothing like him. He never saw the wrong he'd done no matter how many times I told him I was hurting and he clearly saw my tears. You were man enough to apologize and own up to it, however, I need to own up to my part in this, as well. I jumped down your throat and that was wrong of me. I stormed out without staying here and talking it out. I've always tried to avoid confrontations, but that's no excuse. We have to communicate."

"No, you needed your space, and I understand that you were scared history was repeating itself, but it's not. I just hope that we're on the same page. You're it for me. I've finally found my soul mate. My equal. The one woman I can honestly say I'm in love with, and I can't see myself with anyone else but you, Blythe."

Blythe rested her hands on either side of his face and kissed the lips that she craved and missed so much. "I love you, too. Very much, Prez, and I can't see myself with anyone else, either."

Rising from his spot on the floor, he moved next to her and set her on his lap. Hope bounced over carrying the bone in her mouth, dropped it and placed one of her paws on Blythe's leg in an affectionate manner.

"I think Hope agrees with our decision. She saw how mopey I was these past few days. She missed you, as well. You left your Paint, Sip, Chat T-shirt here, and she's been carrying it around and searching for you. She even slept on your chaise lounge last night."

Blythe petted her head. "Aw, how sweet. You missed me, pretty girl? I missed you and your daddy very much."

Hope barked before lying back on the floor and chewing on her bone once more.

"Do you want to open one of your gifts right now?" Preston asked.

"I'd love to. And I have yours, too." She slid off his lap and headed toward the elevator to retrieve his gift.

"Meet me by the tree."

Moments later, they sat in front of the tree, and Blythe was giddy as well as curious what he was going to give her for Christmas. She hadn't hinted at anything, but Prez was creative, and she had a feeling he'd put a lot of thought into it, as he did everything else.

"Close your eyes and hold out your hand."

She started to giggle but did as instructed. "Goodness, I'm nervous." She sensed him move away from her when a whiff of his cologne flew past her nose. "Preston, did you leave?"

"Keep your eyes shut, baby girl." He yelled it out, and she sensed he was in one of the rooms down the hallway.

"Okay, hurry up. I'm excited," she squealed, bouncing up and down on the floor.

Seconds later, she felt something squirmy and warm in her hands and screamed out a laugh as she opened her eyes to see a golden retriever puppy with sweet brown eyes whimpering and staring at her.

"Oh, my goodness. It's a puppy. A cute little puppy." She nuzzled it against her and then lifted it up to see what the sex was. "Oh, he's a boy, and so cute."

"He's all yours. He's ten weeks old. Shots are all updated, and he just needs a name. I've been calling him Sport, but you can name him whatever you like, and I'll get it engraved on his tag."

"How did you know this is the only thing I wanted for Christmas?"

"You'd mentioned when you met Hope that you wanted another dog. I saw this little fellow where Hope trains, and I knew he'd be perfect for you. He's actually a distant relative of Hope's."

"Aw, and he is adorable. I love the name Sport, and I think he does, too," she decided as his ears perked up at hearing his name. She put him down and rubbed his belly, which he seemed to enjoy.

"I also have everything you'll need for him. Training crate, bed, food, toys and treats."

"Oh, my, thank you." She handed the puppy to Preston and rose. "Let me go grab your gift from behind the tree. Close your eyes."

Moments later, she set the wrapped painting in front of him. "Okay, open them."

Opening his eyes, Preston grinned wide as he ripped the bow and wrapping paper off to expose a painting of him reading to the children at the hospital with Hope lying at his feet. "Wow...when did you...? How? This is wonderful."

"I took several pictures of you while you read to the children. I was going to send you the pics, but I know how much you love paintings."

"This is beautiful. Thank you. I think this is the best Christmas ever." He placed the painting next to the couch and pulled her down to the floor with him. "I can't wait to spend many, many more with you." He imprisoned her lips with his in an unhurried, engaging kiss that eventually ended with them intertwined and naked by the fireplace.

Epilogue

A year later

Preston bobbed his head to the sounds of the Braxton Chase Quartet on New Year's Eve at Braxton's club. All of the Chase family and committee members were present for the appreciation celebration after the second annual Winter Wonderland project, which was bigger and more extravagant than the first.

Preston had never been happier than he was at that moment. He had his arm wrapped around the waist of the woman of his dreams, who chatted with Tiffani as they sat in a VIP booth with a perfect view of the stage. Every now and then, Blythe would kiss his cheek or his lips. He loved her so much, it was inevitable to him of what he planned to do that evening.

He snickered to himself as he thought about how over a year ago, at the christening brunch for Megan's twin daughters, Braxton had pointed out that Blythe Ventura could be the one. Preston had laughed it off but found himself staring at her for the rest of the afternoon. That wasn't uncommon when he saw her at events with Tiffani or ran into her at the bakery. He'd never been able to take his eyes off her and always found a reason to speak or flirt with her. And while a part of him had wanted to ask her out, he knew he wasn't ready for a woman like Blythe. She was the kind of woman you introduced to your mother and one day married. Now he was ready. He had to make her all his for the rest of their lives.

Preston placed his focus on the stage as Braxton hit the last note of "'Round Midnight" on his grand piano, which sat center stage. Standing, he made his way to the front of the stage with his microphone. He gave Preston a knowing glance before speaking to the crowd.

"Alright, it's about that time, ladies and gentlemen. Just a few more moments before midnight. Make sure to grab your loved ones." Braxton made his way to Elle, who stood just below the stage, holding their daughter, Bree, and pulled them close to him.

Preston laid a kiss to Blythe's bare shoulder as she

giggled. "Ready for the new year and all the exciting adventures that await us?"

"Mmm-hmm. Indeed I am. You're going to be in it again, right?"

"For sure. I wouldn't miss it. I enjoyed this past year, getting to know all of your cute quirks. I intend never to miss a single year with the most beautiful woman in the world." He kissed the same spot again and ran his lips to the side of her neck, which always produced a sultry moan from her. "Alright, woman, you're making me forget we're in a public place, but I do have the pass code to the back offices."

She giggled again and pinched his cheek. "Let's go join your family on the dance floor for the champagne toast."

Minutes later, the big countdown began, and at midnight, he grabbed Blythe for a long, deep kiss. He once again forgot they were in a public place as his lips joined with her tantalizing, kissable ones, but he didn't care. He had his woman in his arms, and life couldn't get any better, except that it could and it would soon.

Pulling her away from the crowd, he led her to a photo booth set up in the lobby area.

Blythe started to grin when she saw it. "Oh, I don't remember seeing this when we entered. We could've taken pictures then."

Shrugging lightly, he pulled back the curtain and motioned for her to get in. "You wanna make another memory?" he questioned as she slid in, followed by him. Pulling the curtain shut, he turned to face her. Her eyes were wide like saucers.

"Prez…right here, with everyone we know just a few feet away? And people passing by?"

"Um…you do remember the Christmas party at Tiffani's last year and this past summer at Megan's home in the Hamptons? Right?"

"Baby…"

"No, I'm teasing, but let's hurry up and take pictures before the rest of the crowd begins to do the same."

"And then we can leave and go home?" she asked with a devilish expression. "I have something for you that I think you're going to enjoy."

"Oh, yeah? Alright, I'll push the button, so get ready."

She ran her fingers through her curly hair and sat up straight. "Ready."

He pushed the button. The first flash went off a few seconds later. He posed with her and then dropped to his knee and pulled a black velvet box out of his tuxedo jacket pocket. Confusion washed over her face and then was replaced with excitement as she started to laugh and cry at the same time. Preston opened the box, and she saw a gorgeous five-carat, flawless, princess-cut diamond ring. Blythe's happy tears streamed down her face, and the tears in his own eyes flowed.

"Blythe, I love you. Love you more than I thought possible. For years I searched for the right woman to love and cherish. To take care of and to appreciate. I think I've known all along you were meant to be mine and I was meant to be yours. I remember when I first laid eyes on you, thinking, 'Damn, she's one bad woman. I bet her man worships the ground she walks on.' And I was right, because I do, and there's nothing I wouldn't do for you, baby girl. You know that. You're the one I want to marry, have children with, and of course take care of our beloved dogs with."

He took the ring out the box and slid it on her finger as her hands shook and she cried harder.

"Blythe Rosa Ventura, will you do me the honor of being my wife?"

"Yes…yes, John Preston Chase III, I would love to be your wife until death do us part."

"Yes, she said yes!" Preston shouted before snatching her to him for a kiss.

"I had no idea this would to happen," she said, gazing back and forth between him and the ring. "Wait, did you ask my parents?"

"Yep, yesterday when I picked them up from the airport. We had lunch and discussed it. That's why I volunteered to pick them up…oh, and why I had Ms. Bernice at the last minute tell you she wasn't able to do the paint party for you."

"Oh, my goodness, she knows?"

"Yep. So does Braxton. I had to arrange it with his event coordinator to have the photo booth placed here for a few moments. In fact, it's going to my home tomorrow so we can always remember this special moment and all the others we've had in photo booths."

Giggling, she kissed his cheek, and they slid out of the booth. Their pictures were waiting at the bottom of the developing tray. She grabbed them and began to flip through while laughing.

"Oh, my goodness, look at me. Was I crying that hard?" Wiping her tears, she flipped through the dozens of pictures that commemorated the proposal. "These are perfect."

"Yeah, well, I figured that would be a great way to ask you in private but still have the pictures for our memories. Besides, we have this thing for photo booths," he said with a wink.

"Who else knows? Tiffani? Does she know?"

"For sure. She helped pick out your ring. You know your girl looks out for you."

"That would explain why she was really bubbly and chatty earlier. I thought the champagne had gone to her head, but she only had bubbling apple cider…" Blythe's hand flew to her mouth. "Oh, my goodness! Oh, my goodness! Now that I think about it, she only had water at Christmas dinner."

"Mmm-hmm… I noticed that, too, but didn't think much of it until you just said it. So, you think I'm going to be an uncle again?"

"She has been glowing lately."

He kissed her forehead. "Like you are now."

"That's because I'm happy to be with you, my fiancé. Oh, I love the way that sounds. Let's go tell everyone our wonderful news."

Later on that night, they lay intertwined on one of their favorite chaise lounges in front of the fireplace. Hope and Sport, who were expecting puppies, were lying on the opposite chaise. Blythe was still in awe over the unexpected proposal and her gorgeous rock. Their families had been overjoyed for them and for Tiffani, who announced she was four months pregnant with a girl.

"Are you asleep, baby girl?" he asked in a sleepy tone, followed by a yawn.

"I should be, considering it's almost four in the morning, but I'm wired."

"How do you feel about short engagements? Because I want to marry you as soon as possible."

"I couldn't agree more. How about this spring around Easter?"

"That will work."

"And I have a crazy idea, too." She bounced up and sat crisscross at the end of the chaise.

"What's that?"

"Well, last year, before you took me skydiving for the first time, I did so much extensive research, viewed tons of videos and pictures. But the ones I remembered the most were of people actually getting married while skydiving. That would be the coolest thing ever. And we have so much fun when we go."

Preston sat all the way up and stared at her in shock. "I can't believe you just suggested that. I've always thought it would be a cool idea, too, but I figured whoever I married probably wouldn't go for it. This just proves more and more that we're soul mates, baby girl. Goodness, how did I live my life before you?"

"You were miserable," she teased, kissing his cheek. "Sooo...you think we should do it, too?"

"Oh, most definitely. We just have to work out the kinks. My first instructor is also an ordained minister and does wedding ceremonies in the air often. I'll give him a call."

Blythe grabbed her cell phone from the floor where her dress lay along with his clothes, and opened it to the notepad app to take notes. "Okay, so we probably will need two ceremonies because all of our families aren't going to jump with us. Luckily your dad and my dad will, which is great because I'll need my dad to give me away somehow in the sky. However, our mothers aren't jumping, but perhaps we can convince them at least to be in the plane."

"Oh, yeah, I agree."

"So, the second one will be more traditional. I briefly talked with Elle earlier about my wedding dress, but I can't jump in it."

"I want you to have your dream wedding, too. I'm all for both, baby girl. I've kinda pictured it both ways."

"Perfect. We'll skydive first and then have the traditional ceremony in the next day or two? Or traditional first and then jump?"

"Does that include two honeymoons? Just kidding…sort of…but it could be a weekend of festivities. That way, family members and close friends won't have so many save-the-dates."

"That's a great idea, Prez," she agreed, typing everything he said. "What else?"

"We can have the first ceremony in the sky, and whoever wants to jump with us can. I know Sydney, Bryce, Braxton and Elle will since they've gone with us before. Steven and Broderick, maybe. Megan and Tiffani, no, and not because they're pregnant. They're scared of heights. Sasha and Devin, for sure. All my Arrington cousins and their spouses, yes, except for Shelbi, since she's pregnant again. Otherwise she would, considering that she has before. Your sisters, maybe. Hope and Sport, yes, they've been with us before. We just have to wait until after Hope has her puppies and the vet gives the approval. Everyone else can wait below at the observation deck."

"And then we can have an intimate dinner party or rehearsal dinner and the next day get married all over again. Yippie!"

Drawing her into his arms, he kissed her gently

on the lips. "Babe, I've been chasing the dream of love for years, and I never felt so complete before I found you. I love you, baby girl."

"And I love you, Prez. Can we go skydiving tomorrow?"

Preston chuckled and kissed her again. He'd definitely found the woman of his dreams.

* * * * *

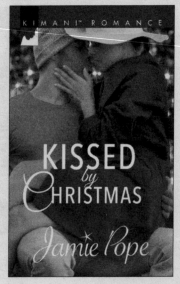

*From the very
first touch…*

NANA PRAH

*A Perfect
Caress*

When businessman Dante Sanderson brushes hands with Lanelle
Murphy, he can't get her out of his head. Lanelle is sure their sparks
mean another heartache. From charity-ball dances to strolls in
Milan, desire pushes her into his arms. Will she be able to seize this
second chance at love?

Available December 2016!

REQUEST YOUR FREE BOOKS!

2 FREE NOVELS PLUS 2 FREE GIFTS!

KIMANI™ ROMANCE

Love's ultimate destination!

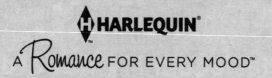

JUST CAN'T GET ENOUGH?

Join our social communities
and talk to us online.

You will have access to the latest
news on upcoming titles and special
promotions, but most importantly,
you can talk to other fans about your
favorite Harlequin reads.

Harlequin.com/Community

Facebook.com/HarlequinBooks

Twitter.com/HarlequinBooks

Pinterest.com/HarlequinBooks